"You Have My Baby."

Lucy swallowed against a rising sense of panic. "No. I have *my* baby. It's still as much mine, no matter who fathered it. And while I can understand that you're upset—" she blinked at the fury that suddenly darkened Andrew's eyes to slate "—very upset," she amended, "there's nothing I can do about it."

"You can let me have my child. No, hear me out," Andrew added as he saw her eyes widen in disbelief at his suggestion. "Miss Day had agreed to carry my child to term for the sum of twenty thousand dollars. I'll give you the same amount."

"What I'd like to give you is a good swift smack alongside the head," she sputtered angrily. "How dare you try to buy my baby!"

"It's mine, too." Andrew's voice rose. "That baby has half my genetic code."

"Well, I hope she didn't get the half for brains or she's in deep trouble."

Dear Reader:

Welcome to the world of Silhouette Desire. Join me as we travel to a land of incredible passion and tantalizing romance—a place where dreams can, and do, come true.

When I read a Silhouette Desire, I sometimes feel as if I'm going on a little vacation. I can relax, put my feet up, and be transported to a new world...a world that has, naturally, a perfect hero just waiting to whisk me away! These are stories to remember, containing moments to treasure.

Silhouette Desire novels are romantic love stories— sensuous yet emotional. As a reader, you not only see the hero and heroine fall in love, you also feel what they're feeling.

Look for books by some of your favorite Silhouette Desire authors: Joan Hohl, BJ James, Linda Lael Miller and Diana Palmer.

So enjoy!

Lucia Macro
Senior Editor

JUDITH McWILLIAMS

THAT'S MY BABY

SILHOUETTE *Desire*

Published by Silhouette Books New York

America's Publisher of Contemporary Romance

SILHOUETTE BOOKS
300 East 42nd St., New York, N.Y. 10017

ISBN: 0-373-05597-8

First Silhouette Books printing October 1990

Printed in the U.S.A.

Books by Judith McWilliams

Silhouette Desire

Reluctant Partners #441
A Perfect Season #545
That's My Baby #597

Silhouette Romance

Gift of the Gods #479

JUDITH McWILLIAMS

began to enjoy romances while in search of the proverbial "happily ever afters." But she always found herself rewriting the endings, and eventually the beginnings, of the books she read. Then her husband finally suggested that she write novels of her own, and she's been doing so ever since. An ex-teacher with four children, Judith has traveled the country extensively with her husband and has been greatly influenced by those experiences. But while not tending the garden or caring for family, Judith does what she enjoys most—writing. She has also written under the name Charlotte Hines.

One

"Lucy?" Annie stuck her graying head through the doorway and peered shortsightedly around the poorly lit storeroom.

"Over here, Annie." A voice issued from behind a huge stack of boxes a second before a cheerful face framed by shiny brown curls appeared above them.

"Lucy, you'll never guess what I just sold." Annie threaded her way around the boxes. "Never in a million years."

"Let me think." Lucy's slender fingers made a gesture in front of her that was reminiscent of a carnival fortune-teller's over a crystal ball. She squinted down into the imaginary globe and intoned in sepulchral tones, "I see yarn."

"Well, of course you see yarn," Annie said impatiently. "This is a yarn store. The whole place is filled with yarn."

She gestured around the room with its open boxes filled with brightly colored skeins.

"You are disrupting my concentration," Lucy complained in a fractured gypsy accent. "I see pale cream yarn." She gestured again with her hands as if trying to clear the mist. "I see lots of pale cream alpaca yarn. Sixty-three skeins, to be exact. Worsted weight," she added with a twinkle in her warm brown eyes.

Annie's mouth fell open. "You peeked while I was ringing up the sale," she accused.

"Nope," Lucy grinned. "I answered the phone this morning when the lady called to see if we carried alpaca yarn, and I also figured out how much she needed for her project."

"She must be making a sweater for an elephant," Annie muttered. "But at twelve-fifty a skein, I hope she outfits the whole herd. Do you realize she paid cash? The total was eight hundred forty-two dollars and sixty-three cents, and she plunked down nine one-hundred-dollar bills." Annie shook her head in amazement.

"Drat!" Lucy frowned. "Put the bills under the money drawer with the checks, and I'll deposit them in the bank when I see the builder at lunchtime. Keeping that much cash in the store is asking for trouble."

"Builder?" Annie repeated. "Do you mean to tell me that you're finally going to do something about this sorry excuse for a storeroom?"

"Yup. I'm going to have it remodeled into a nursery," Lucy said evenly, trying to gauge Annie's reaction. Annie had worked for her since she'd first opened the yarn shop almost ten years ago and she was more than just an employee. She was a friend. A friend whose opinion Lucy valued.

Annie frowned. "A nursery? What do you know about raising plants? You're a needlework expert."

"Not nursery as in plants. Nursery as in baby."

"Baby!" Annie squawked. "You're pregnant?" Her eyes automatically slipped to Lucy's narrow waist.

"Not until this Friday at two."

"You're getting married? But I thought you'd stopped seeing that teacher you were dating."

"I'm not, and I did. I said I was going to get pregnant, not married."

"My God!" Annie sank down on the nearest box and stared at Lucy in shock. "If you aren't going to get married, then how are you going to get pregnant? No, don't answer that." She grimaced. "There's only one way to get pregnant."

"Actually, that's not exactly true," Lucy replied calmly. "There's also artificial insemination."

"Artificial—" Annie gasped. "I have the distinct feeling I'm missing something somewhere. Suppose you start at the beginning and this time throw in a few more facts. Unless it's a secret?"

"No, pregnancy is not something one can keep secret. At least, not for long," she remarked, hoping Annie would understand what she intended to do. If she didn't, it could create a strained working relationship. Lucy took a deep breath, knowing that in the long run, what Annie thought would make no difference to her final decision.

"I'm three months past my thirty-fifth birthday," Lucy began.

"And I'm going to be fifty-seven next month. Labor Day, to be exact," Annie cut in. "Thirty-five seems pretty young to me."

"Not for someone who wants a child. I'm already in the high-risk group for all kinds of birth defects, and every year makes it worse. Pretty soon I'm going to be too old to have kids, no matter what the risk. And I want them. At least one."

"So get married," Annie advised. "That teacher you were dating earlier this summer would have married you in a flash. He was crazy about you. And not only that, but he was a nice guy."

"Too nice to be married simply because I wanted to use him as a stud. Don deserves a wife who loves him. And much as I liked him, I didn't love him." She sighed. "And God knows, I tried hard enough to fall in love with him."

"You should have married him anyway," Annie insisted. "Love would have come after the wedding."

"More likely, what would have come after would have been regrets and guilt that I couldn't give him what he deserved."

"Listen, Lucy. You take it from one who's been there. Love as a basis for marriage is grossly overrated. I got married at eighteen because I was so much in love I couldn't bear the thought of not doing so. Unfortunately, once our hormones cooled off, we found we didn't have a thing in common. We didn't even like each other very much. Life became a constant battle. I couldn't live with him, and I couldn't live without him. Believe me, I would have infinitely preferred being married to someone I liked instead of someone I loved. Of course, I was sorry when he had that massive heart attack and died, but the peace has been lovely."

"There has to be more to love than a rush of hormones to the head," Lucy insisted. "Real love includes shared interests and similar philosophical outlooks on life."

"Your problem is that you read too much." Annie nodded sagely. "Real life isn't perfect. You settle for what you can get and build on that."

"I refuse to settle for anything. Besides, what if you're wrong and I'm right? Suppose there really is a perfect man for me out there somewhere but I go ahead and marry Don and have my family. And then I meet Mr. Right. What do I do? Break up a marriage with a nice man and deprive my kids of their father so that I can be happy? Or keep the family intact and go through life knowing that I could have had so much more if I'd just been patient awhile longer?"

"But suppose this perfect lover never does come along? Then what?" Annie demanded.

"Then I'll remain single. I have no problems with that. I like my life. I have a wide circle of friends. I own a prosperous yarn shop that not only supports me in comfort but also provides me with a great deal of personal satisfaction. The only flaw in staying single as far as I can see is not having children, and I'm taking steps to remedy that."

"But, Lucy, suppose you do go through with this and have the kid and then meet Mr. Right? What's he going to say?"

"If he's Mr. Right, he'll understand. If he doesn't, who needs him?"

"I give up!" Annie threw her hands up in defeat. "You're an impossible romantic."

"No." Lucy shook her head. "What I am is eminently practical. I've faced the fact that every year that passes makes it less likely I'll find someone to marry. So I'm going to make the best of it."

"Well, it'll be kind of nice to have a baby around here, although this place is depressing enough to give him a complex." She glanced around the room with distaste.

"Or her. Don't worry, the builder'll take care of that. And don't forget to put a couple of skeins of that alpaca yarn aside in case our customer doesn't knit to gauge and runs short."

"Will do," Annie agreed. "Who knows, she might decide to expand into camel hair next."

Lucy chuckled. "We should be so lucky. I think I'm just going to admit defeat and put the stuff on sale because..."

She broke off as the tinkling chimes signaled the arrival of another customer.

"I'll get that." Annie hurried out of the storeroom.

Lucy watched her go and then slowly sank back down on one of the boxes, feeling drained. She wasn't positive that what she was about to do was the right thing. But she honestly didn't see what options she had. Not if she wanted a child. And she did. A soft smile curved her lips at the thought of a baby—of someone of her own to love and be loved by. It would work out for the best, she told herself. No matter what it took, she'd make it work.

Lucy's determination didn't falter despite the fact that Annie had gone out of her way to locate and show her every article she could find on the perils of single parenthood. Oddly enough, they had the effect of strengthening Lucy's resolve. Not only did she come to realize that literally millions of women were struggling to raise children on their own, but the vast majority of the problems they faced didn't apply to her. She wasn't going to have to worry about what the landlord might say about an infant, because she owned her own home. Day care would not be a problem as she intended to keep the baby with her at the shop. Finances weren't an issue as she not only earned a modestly luxurious living from her business, but she also had a healthy and growing investment portfolio—the basis of which had been inherited from her parents. And while she wouldn't have the emotional support of a husband, neither would she have to cope with the aftermath of a bitter divorce and custody fight or the potentially traumatic effects of shuffling a child back and forth between two homes and two life-styles.

Thus, Lucy was able to approach her appointment at the clinic in New York City on Friday with outward calm. But it was a calm that began to crumble when she stepped out of the elevator on the twelfth floor of the Manhattan Professional Building. She expelled her breath on a long, slow sigh, trying to control her mounting nervousness.

Just hang in there, she encouraged herself. All you have to do is get through the next hour, and with any luck at all you'll never have to come back again.

She smoothed her hand down over her cream linen skirt, checked to make sure her jade silk blouse was buttoned and then twitched the suit jacket into place. Taking a deep breath, she pushed open the door to the obstetrics clinic and walked in, coming to a halt as a wave of noise seemed to roll over her. She looked around the office in dismay. It was packed. Not only was every seat taken, but several children were sitting on the floor. In the corner under an end table a pudgy toddler was methodically eating a magazine while his obviously pregnant mother ignored him. Across from him a wan-looking woman was holding a very young infant who was shrieking at the top of its lungs. The woman shifted the baby to her other shoulder but the crying didn't stop.

Lucy gave her a sympathetic smile and turned toward the reception desk. There was no one there. She peered down the hallway behind it, wondering what had happened. During her first visit two months ago, she'd shared the waiting room with only two other women and had been ushered in to see her doctor exactly on time.

"So sorry." An agitated-looking young woman in a white uniform emerged from the hallway and hurried over to the desk.

"No problem," Lucy replied soothingly. "My name is Lucy Hartford, and I have a two o'clock appointment with Dr. Wycliff."

"Actually, there is a problem." The woman sighed. "Both Dr. Wycliff and Dr. Quinton are at the hospital delivering babies. Dr. LeDonne is seeing both their patients as well as his own—which has created a bit of a backlog." She gestured wearily toward the waiting room. "The appointments are running about forty-five minutes late."

"I don't mind waiting. One expects a few delays in an obstetrician's office."

"Fine." The nurse gave her a harried smile. "Then, if you'll just have a seat, the doctor'll get to you just as soon as he can."

As Lucy glanced around the packed room, her gaze was unexpectedly caught and held by a pair of bright blue eyes set in a ruggedly masculine face. She watched in surprise as the man got to his feet and, stepping aside, gestured toward his now empty seat.

The very novelty of a man giving up his seat in New York City held her immobile for a second, and she stared at him in surprise. The impatience darkening his incredible blue eyes prodded her into action, and with a warm smile Lucy crossed the room and sat down beside the woman he was obviously with.

Surreptitiously, Lucy glanced at the young woman, watching as her long, white fingers kept clenching and unclenching. Her *ringless*, long, white, fingers, Lucy noted, wondering what the relationship between them was. Covertly she studied the man from beneath her lashes. He was leaning up against the wall beside her with a lithe grace that bespoke a well-conditioned body. A well-constructed one, too, she thought with an instinctive surge of feminine appreciation for a truly masculine-looking man.

The light gray suit he was wearing had obviously been handmade for him, as had the leather shoes that encased his slightly oversize feet. His burgundy tie glowed against the pristine whiteness of his shirt like a polished jewel. But it was his face which held her attention. Its roughly hewed planes with its high cheekbones and hawklike nose weren't conventionally handsome, but they reflected the force of the vibrant personality behind them. That it was a powerful personality Lucy had no doubt as her eyes lingered on the uncompromising jut of his chin. As he ran his long, tanned fingers through his inky black hair, she caught a glimpse of a wafer-thin gold watch nestled against the dark hairs on his wrist.

Whatever else he was, he was a man of considerable financial resources—resources he did not appear to have shared with the woman with him. Lucy studied her well-worn jeans and baggy sweater, frowning slightly as she noticed the nervous, almost frightened manner in which the young woman kept watching him. She was too young for him, Lucy thought. And not just physically; she actually appeared afraid of him.

Finally, almost an hour later, a nurse stuck her head into the reception room and said, "Miss Hartford, Miss Day, and Mrs. Acton, would you please follow me?"

Lucy tensed, not caring that she now had a name to put to the young woman—Miss Day. She was on the brink of achieving something she'd always wanted—a baby—and the emotion uppermost in her mind was one of panic. After today, if things worked out the way they were supposed to, her life would be irrevocably changed. For the better, she told herself staunchly as she followed the visibly trembling Miss Day and the very pregnant Mrs. Acton through the door.

"Here you are." The nurse checked their names, handed them their medical charts and pointed down the long hallway. "Use the three empty examining rooms at the end. Someone will be with you in a minute. I hope," she muttered under her breath.

Lucy clutched her chart and followed Miss Day down the hallway while Mrs. Acton paused to ask the nurse something.

They were almost to the examining rooms when Miss Day suddenly spun around, cannoning into Lucy.

Lucy dropped her chart and grabbed for the wall to steady herself.

"What's wrong?" Lucy asked, eyeing the woman's chalk-white face with compassion.

"Nothing." Miss Day hastily picked up their dropped charts and shoved Lucy's at her.

"But—" Lucy glanced back up the corridor. The nurse was still talking to Mrs. Acton.

"I just feel a little sick to my stomach," Miss Day insisted. "I'll just nip into the bathroom till I feel better." She gave Lucy a wobbly smile and scurried away.

Lucy watched her round the corner of the corridor and disappear, wondering if she ought to do something. But what could she do? Morning sickness was a normal consequence of pregnancy and they were in a doctor's office full of health professionals all of whom were far more qualified to deal with the problem than she was.

With a sigh, Lucy absently dropped her chart into the wooden holder beside the door and went inside, hoping the doctor really would be along soon. As nervous as she felt, if she had to wait very long, she'd be following Miss Day to the bathroom.

Lucy sat down on the beige plastic chair at the foot of the examining table and focused on a framed print of a laughing baby. The sight cheered her, helping her to focus on her reason for being here.

Fifteen minutes later, there was a quick rap on the door before it was pushed open to admit a middle-aged nurse who gave her a harried smile.

"Good afternoon." Lucy dredged up a social pleasantry.

The nurse sighed. "It certainly hasn't been so far. If you'll just take your suit jacket off, I'll get your blood pressure before I weigh you."

Lucy obediently slipped it off and, pushing up the sleeve of her silk blouse, held out her arm. "I weigh about a hundred and ten," she offered.

"Nothing personal, dear, but we never take anyone's word for what they weigh. If I had a dollar for every time a patient has shaved ten pounds off their weight...?" She finished taking Lucy's blood pressure and tossed the cuff on the desk behind her. "Up on the scale with you."

"What was my blood pressure?" Lucy asked.

"One-fifty over seventy-eight," she muttered as she slid the metal disk to the right, nodding approvingly when it balanced at one hundred and seven.

"A hundred and fifty?" Lucy repeated in dismay.

"Calm down," the woman said soothingly. "The bottom number's the relevant one and that's great. The top figure fluctuates with how stressed out you happen to be feeling. And most people feel pretty uptight when they visit the doctor. If you were to sit quietly for half an hour or so, it would come right down, although where you'd find a quiet spot in this zoo..."

Taking a paper gown out of the drawer, she handed it to Lucy. "Put that on and climb up on the examining table. The doctor'll be with you just as soon as he can."

Lucy watched the nurse leave, her nerves tightening at the thought of the unknown doctor. The one she'd seen originally had been so nice and reasonable. He'd listened to her request, asked a few pertinent questions about the state of her health and her finances and then said that the only hesitation he had was that he was afraid that she might be making a spur-of-the-moment decision that she'd come to regret. He'd gone on to say that if she still felt the same way in two months time, he'd be glad to help her.

Lucy had been impatient at the delay, but she'd finally decided that in the long run it might be quicker to simply abide by his restrictions because she didn't know where else to go. Her own doctor was an elderly, old-fashioned individual who would never have agreed to her plan. She'd only known about this clinic because it had been mentioned in a newspaper article on surrogate motherhood she'd read. Lucy had correctly assumed that if the clinic was willing to work with surrogates, they'd also be willing to work with a single parent.

So she'd swallowed her impatience and waited the two months, and now her waiting was about to pay off. She felt a heady rush of excitement as she slipped on the paper gown, which crackled as she climbed onto the examining table.

She stifled a nervous giggle as she remembered a friend of hers who'd said that the first thing to go in her pregnancy hadn't been her figure, it had been her modesty.

After another twenty-minute wait, the nurse bustled in.

"Lie back on the table while I drape you," she ordered, pulling a sheet out of the drawer.

Lucy lay down, struggling to act like the calm, professional woman she knew herself to be. Her facade cracked slightly as a white-coated man rushed in.

"Hi, I'm Dr. LeDonne. Sorry to keep you waiting, but it's been one of those days. Now, then—" he rushed on before she could insert a social pleasantry "—are you still of the same mind?"

"Yes," Lucy answered emphatically.

"And you do realize that the clinic accepts no responsibility if there is a problem with the baby?"

"Yes. Dr. Wycliff explained it all," Lucy said impatiently, wishing he'd stop acting like a lawyer and start acting like the doctor he was.

"Just wanted to be sure you understood beforehand, dear." He patted her shoulder. "It saves a lot of trouble in the long run." He took a syringe out of the pan the nurse held out to him. "Ignorance and misunderstanding can lead to all kinds of problems. Now, if you'll just relax we'll get on with it.''

Relax! Lucy thought wildly. She was so tense she felt as if she were about to shatter into a million pieces. She also felt an underlying sense of sadness. Babies were supposed to be created through an act of love, and this was all so coldly clinical. But it didn't matter, she assured herself. No matter what the baby's inception, it would be loved. Loved with all her heart.

''There you are, dear.'' The doctor dropped the now empty syringe into the metal pan with a clatter. ''Just lie perfectly still for a while and I'll be back with some instructions before you leave.'' He gave her a distracted smile and hurried out, trailed by the nurse, leaving Lucy prey to a confusing mass of emotions—relief that it was over, intense joy that she might be going to have a baby, fear of the whole idea of motherhood, and trepidation that it might not work and she would have to go through all this again next month.

After what seemed like an age to Lucy's jumpy nerves, the nurse returned and said, ''You can get dressed now. Doctor'll be in in a few minutes.''

Lucy scrambled off the rock-hard examining table. Now that it was over, all she wanted was to leave—to forget where her baby had come from and concentrate on the baby itself.

To her relief, the doctor showed no inclination to detain her. He hurried in, gave her a list of instructions headed by a lurid warning of the horrors that might befall her developing baby if she took any medication without first checking with her own physician, and ending with the request that she phone them in a month and let them know if she was going to need another appointment.

Lucy listened carefully, nodded in agreement, and then, picking up her purse, started to leave.

"Thank you, Doctor." She paused in the open doorway.

"Glad to be of assistance, Miss Day."

"Hartford," Lucy automatically corrected him, and then wished she hadn't when she saw the horrified expression chase across his face. Obviously, he felt it was a reflection on his professional competence that he'd forgotten a patient's name, although she didn't see why he should when she wasn't even his patient.

She gave him a warm smile to show she wasn't offended and hurried out, planning on spending the rest of the afternoon looking through New York City's baby shops for ideas for decorating her nursery.

Six weeks later she was back in the city, and this time she intended to do more than just look at the shops. She grinned at her reflection in the polished bronze doors of the elevator, so happy she could barely contain the feeling. Just as soon as she got this visit to the obstetrics clinic out of the way, she was going to visit F.A.O. Schwarz's toy store.

She frowned as she got off the elevator on the twelfth floor, wondering why this visit was even necessary. When she'd called the clinic the week before to tell them that her own doctor had just confirmed her pregnancy, Dr. Wycliff had asked her to come in. In fact, he'd been most insistent. Insistent to the point where she'd felt like asking him if her check had bounced.

Ah, well, Lucy thought, whatever it was that Dr. Wycliff wanted shouldn't take long, and she did owe him something. Without him, she wouldn't be pregnant.

Lucy opened the door to the clinic and stepped into a rerun of her last visit. The room was packed. Sighing, she headed toward the reception desk to check in, prepared for a long wait. To her surprise, the minute she gave her name she was immediately ushered to Dr. Wycliff's office.

Lucy frowned, trying to ignore the frisson of unease that chased over her skin. Why was she getting preference over all those people in the waiting room? Unless, perhaps, it was because her visit wasn't going to take long? Maybe there was simply some form or other he'd forgotten to have her sign.

"If you'll just go in, Miss Hartford." The young nurse opened the door to Dr. Wycliff's office and gave Lucy an encouraging smile.

Lucy smiled back and entered the luxurious office. Her smile slipped slightly as she suddenly found herself the focus of three pairs of masculine eyes.

Her glance skimmed over the two doctors she'd dealt with previously to land on the third man. She frowned as her gaze became entangled in his bright blue eyes. He looked vaguely familiar. As if... Of course—her memory clicked into place. He was the man who'd been in the waiting room with that young woman six weeks ago. His "significant other," if their lack of rings was anything to go by. But why was he here? Unless the nurse had shown her to the wrong office?

Feeling socially gauche under the three men's riveting stares, she asked, "Am I in the right office?"

"Forgive me, Miss Hartford." Dr. Wycliff gestured toward the empty chair beside the man. "Won't you please sit down?"

"You must be wondering what this is all about." Dr. LeDonne tried for a jovial grin, which sat oddly on his tense features.

What was going on here? Lucy began to pick up some of the tension in the room and her stomach rolled protestingly. She took a deep breath and swallowed against the sensation, sending up a silent prayer that her stomach would behave. A queasy stomach had been her first indication that she was pregnant, but until now the nausea had been confined to early morning.

"You met Dr. LeDonne when you visited us in August, and this is Andrew Killion, another patient of ours." Dr. Wycliff nodded toward the man beside her.

Lucy took Andrew's outstretched hand, shivering slightly as his warm fingers closed possessively over hers. His eyes glowed with some suppressed emotion she couldn't quite put a name to, but it still made her uneasy. Something was wrong here. Something was very wrong. Telling herself she was being fanciful, she gently tugged her hand free and turned back to Dr. Wycliff.

"You're probably curious as to why we asked you to come in today," he continued.

"Yes, I am," she replied dryly wondering if he ever intended to get to the point.

"It's really my fault," Dr. LeDonne cut in. "Or, more accurately, the fault of the medical chart you had. How on earth did you wind up with Miss Day's chart? Our receptionist swears she gave you the right one."

"Miss Day?" That was the name he'd called her when she'd been leaving last time, Lucy remembered. So that's why he'd made the mistake.

"Miss Day was the young woman you were with?" Lucy asked Andrew Killion.

"Yes," he clipped out.

"Then I know what happened." Lucy smiled at the three men. "She bumped into me halfway to the examining rooms and when we picked up our charts they must have gotten mixed up."

"You didn't think to check?" Andrew demanded.

"Forgive me," she said wryly. "I had a lot on my mind at the time. Besides, I don't see what all the fuss is about. Simply transfer the medical information from her chart to mine."

Dr. Wycliff took off his glasses and rubbed the bridge of his nose. "You don't understand, Miss Hartford. Miss Day had agreed to act as a surrogate mother for Mr. Killion here."

Surrogate mother! Lucy stared at Andrew Killion in surprise, wondering why he had hired a surrogate. He looked as if he could have his pick of women only too eager to marry him and give him children in the conventional manner.

"Apparently Miss Day changed her mind and left through the rear door, and in the confusion no one noticed," Dr. LeDonne explained.

"Well, I'm sorry. But I still don't see what all this has to do with me," Lucy said.

"I had already collected the specimen from Mr. Killion and was on my way to Miss Day. I read the name on your chart, assumed you were Miss Day and...and used Mr. Killion's sperm instead of an anonymous donor's," Dr. LeDonne finished in a rush.

Lucy stared at him in horror as the truth ricocheted through her stunned mind with the force of a rifle shot. A chill iced her skin and her stomach heaved as the ramifications of what had happened swirled through her. She wasn't pregnant by a safely anonymous donor. Her baby's father suddenly had a face and a name. Her breath was suspended in her lungs, and she could literally feel the blood draining from her cheeks. Dr. LeDonne's features wavered slightly and there was an ominous buzzing in her ears.

Strangely enough, it was Andrew and not one of the two doctors who realized what was happening to her.

His large hand closed around the back of her neck and he pushed her head down. "Take shallow breaths," he ordered.

Lucy tried to comply, but the feel of his hard fingers burning into her icy skin interfered with her thought processes, confusing her further.

"I'm all right now," she gasped weakly. "I'm not going to faint."

Andrew grasped her chin and tilted her head back. His eyes traced over her pale features, watching in satisfaction as the rush of blood beneath her fair skin brought some color in its wake.

"Sorry," she muttered, leaning back and breaking the unsettling contact.

"I realize this has been a shock, Miss Hartford," Dr. Wycliff said, "but... Well, you can see that this leaves us in a real bind. I mean, Mr. Killion here..." He gestured helplessly.

"What he means is that you have my baby," Andrew stated flatly.

Lucy swallowed against a rising sense of panic. "No. I have my baby. It's still as much mine, no matter who fathered it. And while I can understand that you're upset..." She blinked at the fury that suddenly darkened his eyes to slate. "Very upset," she amended, "there's nothing I can do about it."

"You can let me have my child. No, hear me out," Andrew added as her eyes widened in disbelief at his monstrous suggestion. "Miss Day had agreed to carry my child to term for the sum of twenty thousand dollars. I'll give you the same amount."

"What I'd like to give you is a good swift smack alongside the head," she sputtered angrily. "How dare you try to buy my baby?"

"It's mine, too." Andrew's voice rose. "That baby has half my genetic code."

"Well, I hope she didn't get the half for brains or she's in deep trouble," Lucy snapped, jumping to her feet. This was awful. Her logical, well-thought-out solution to motherhood had suddenly become a minefield, and she felt as if she'd been cut loose in a world she didn't understand and couldn't control. And to make matters worse, she was afraid she was going to throw up.

"Please, Miss Hartford, if you'll just sit back down," Dr. Wycliff began soothingly. "We'll discuss this in a civilized fashion."

"No!" Lucy bit out. "I don't feel the least bit civilized about this. I feel furious! Good-day, gentlemen." She rushed from the office, ignoring Andrew's shouted command to wait. Right now, all she cared about was reaching the public rest rooms by the elevator before she lost her lunch.

Two

"You all right, honey?" A plump, middle-aged woman eyed Lucy worriedly when she finally emerged from the bathroom stall.

"Yes, thank you." Lucy gave the woman a pale smile and glanced into the large mirror above the row of sinks, wincing at what she saw. No wonder the woman looked concerned, Lucy thought in dismay. Her lips were bloodless and her eyes looked like dull coals set in her chalk-white skin. If it was possible, she looked as bad as she felt.

"You sure?" the woman persisted, watching as Lucy splashed water on her face.

Its coldness made Lucy feel fractionally better and she was able to reply with some of her normal vigor, "I really am fine. I'm just pregnant." Despite her worries, she still felt a small thrill of satisfaction in announcing her impending motherhood.

"Oh, if that's all..." The woman beamed at Lucy. "Don't you worry, honey. Another couple of months and it'll all be over. Unless..." She frowned consideringly. "Unless you turn out to be one of those unlucky ones who are sick the whole nine months. Why, I remember with my second one, I was still throwing up when I went to the hospital to have her. Course now, my first husband and I were in the midst of a messy divorce at the time, and they do say that stress makes nausea worse."

"That would probably account for it," Lucy said grimly. Things didn't get much more stressful than having some strange man tell you that your baby was his and he wanted it. She shivered slightly at the memory of the hard gleam in his eyes. Andrew Killion was going to be a problem. No doubt about it. She took a deep, steadying breath and pushed her auburn hair off her forehead. Its rich color provided an incongruous frame for her pinched features.

"You sure you're okay?" the woman repeated.

Lucy blinked, having forgotten the woman was even there.

"Oh, yes," she replied. "I was simply considering what you said about stress making the nausea worse. I didn't know that. I'm going to have to pick up a book on pregnancy."

"Don't do it!" the woman told her emphatically. "You'll simply find out a lot of things you didn't really want to know anyway—like the horrors of gaining too much weight. Although—" she studied the way Lucy's leaf-green linen suit hugged her slender curves "—you'll probably turn out to be one of those women who can eat anything and never gain a pound." She heaved a frankly envious sigh. "If you're sure you're okay..."

"There is something you could do for me if you would," Lucy said slowly. She didn't think Andrew had followed her out of the doctor's office, but she wasn't sure. And in her present shaky state she didn't feel up to dealing with him. "Would you mind looking out the door and seeing if there's a man in the hall?"

"A man?" the woman parroted.

"About six foot, black hair, blue eyes, broad shoulders, wearing a gray suit and probably an unpleasant expression."

"Ah, the source of the stress." The woman laughed. "You wait here. I'd be glad to check." She pushed open the door, stuck her head out and then popped back in.

"You're safe," she announced conspiratorially. "There's not a soul in sight."

"Thanks." Lucy grabbed her purse and hurriedly left.

She had pushed the Down button and was staring blindly at the framed information to the side of the elevator when she suddenly realized what it was—a directory of the building's tenants. She glanced down the list, her eyes stopping when she discovered a law firm purporting to specialize in family law.

That was what she needed, she realized. To talk to someone who knew the legal ins and outs of the situation she'd so unexpectedly found herself in. Her own lawyer in Long Island certainly wouldn't know. His specialty was tax law.

Lucy noted the floor, got into the elevator and pushed the right button. She'd try to see them now; and if they wouldn't see her without an appointment, she could at least make one, she decided, feeling a little better now that she was actually doing something positive about the situation.

She had no trouble finding the law offices, although from the looks of the activity in the reception area, most of New York appeared to be either getting a divorce or signing a prenuptial agreement.

"May I help you?" The receptionist gave her a bright, professional smile.

"I hope so." Lucy smiled back. "I'm afraid I don't have an appointment, but something has just come up and since I was already in the building I thought I'd see if there was any chance I could talk to someone about it."

"Well..." The woman looked uncertain. "We don't normally do that. You see, the lawyers like to have a chance to familiarize themselves with a case first but..." She paused at Lucy's disappointed expression. "What was it you want to consult us about?"

"Custody of my child."

"That would be our Mr. Marton." She checked the appointment book on her desk. "Let me ask him if he can spare you a minute, Ms....?"

"Hartford. Lucy Hartford. And thank you. I really appreciate this." Lucy watched the woman disappear into an office and took a deep breath, willing her stomach to behave. If that lady in the rest room was right and stress really did make the nausea worse, she was in for a long seven months.

The woman emerged from the office and gave Lucy a warm smile. "You're in luck, Ms. Hartford. Mr. Marton says he can give you the fifteen minutes before his next appointment." She gestured to the open door behind her.

Lucy hurriedly entered the office before he could change his mind. A man she assumed was Mr. Marton rose as she approached his desk, and Lucy eyed him uncertainly. He didn't look the least like her idea of a high-powered lawyer. He looked like a teddy bear. But as her eyes met his, she saw the keen intelligence shimmering in them and relaxed slightly.

"Have a seat, Ms. Hartford." He gestured toward the leather chair in front of his desk. "I'm Jeffrey Marton. Peggy said you had a problem?"

"Yes, it's about custody of my baby."

Marton picked up a pencil and asked, "How old is the baby?"

"Forty-three days," Lucy replied promptly.

"And it's a . . ."

Lucy frowned at him uncertainly. "A baby. I told you."

"No, I mean a boy or a girl."

"Well, I won't know that until after it's born, will I?" she asked reasonably.

"But you just said . . ."

"Oh." Lucy flushed. "I thought you meant how pregnant am I. The baby isn't born yet."

"I see." Marton gave her a piercing look and suggested, "Suppose you start at the beginning and tell me about it."

"All right." Lucy succinctly related the whole mess. "Well," she asked when she'd finished, "what do you think?"

"That you have a cut-and-dried lawsuit against the clinic. They are clearly negligent."

"I don't want to sue them," she broke out in frustration. "I don't need money, and I most assuredly don't need the publicity. Can you imagine what the scandal sheets would make of this?" Lucy shuddered. "All I want is my baby."

"But it isn't just your child," he said slowly. "It's also the father's. And since he's as much a victim of this mix-up as you are . . ."

"Are you trying to tell me that he has a claim to my baby?"

"To your baby in the sense that it's the baby of both of you. The laws regarding surrogacy are very sketchy—almost to the point of nonexistence, as a matter of fact. And this isn't really surrogacy. What it is is one hell of a mess." Mr. Marton tugged his earlobe thoughtfully. "My educated guess would be that the courts would set up some form of shared custody. Unless we can prove that the father wouldn't be a fit guardian. Do you know his name?"

"Andrew Killion."

Mr. Marton's eyebrows shot up in surprise. "The architect?"

"I don't know. No one told me what he does for a living."

"About forty, black hair, blue eyes, arrogant expression?"

"That's him." Lucy nodded emphatically.

"That's trouble. Andrew Killion is wealthy, well respected in his field, and active in several charities. We haven't got a hope in hell of convincing a court he'd be an unfit father."

"Great." Lucy swallowed uneasily as her stomach lurched. "So what do you suggest I do?"

"Negotiate," he advised succinctly. "It'll buy us time, and there's always the possibility that once the shock of what's happened wears off, he'll drop his demand for custody."

"Do you think he might?" she asked.

"No." Mr. Marton dashed her hopes. "He obviously wants a child very much, so I wouldn't expect him to suddenly change his mind. But it is a possibility, and we have to consider all of them."

"I see." Lucy sighed.

"My advice to you, Ms. Hartford, is to sit down with Killion and discuss this in a rational manner. Try to work out terms you can live with. Then come back, and we'll put it all in writing, because if you bring in lawyers at this stage the focus is going to be on the lawyers' maneuvering, not on what's necessarily best for your baby."

"You're probably right." Lucy got to her feet, not sure if talking to him had helped or not. Most of what he'd said had been things she hadn't wanted to hear. But at least she now knew exactly where she stood, and just knowing was a relief in a strange way.

"I really appreciate your seeing me on such short notice." She dredged up a smile for him.

"Just remember what I said about trying to work things out with Killion." He walked her to the door.

Mr. Marton's advice was all that kept Lucy from slamming the receiver down in panic when she unsuspectingly answered the phone the following afternoon and found herself talking to Andrew.

"...dinner this evening?" The deep velvety sound of his voice flowed disjointedly through her mind. Much as she wanted to say no, she forced herself to agree.

"Why don't you pick me up at my yarn shop?" she suggested. "It's at—"

"I know where it is," Andrew cut in, leaving Lucy wondering where he'd gotten the information and, more importantly, what else he knew about her. It made her feel vulnerable, especially since all she knew about him was what Mr. Marton had told her.

"We close at five-thirty and it takes me a few minutes to lock up. Say five forty-five?"

"Fine," he said, and then hung up, almost as if he were afraid she might change her mind.

Lucy frowned thoughtfully as she slowly put the receiver down. Could he be as nervous and worried as she was? she wondered. After all, she was the one with possession of the baby, and what was it they said about possession being nine-tenths of the law?

"What's the matter?" Annie eyed her curiously. "You look funny."

"I sure don't feel it." Lucy glanced around to make sure none of her customers was close enough to hear. "I was just talking to the man who made my pregnancy possible."

Annie frowned. "I thought you were using an anonymous donor."

"Anonymity isn't what it used to be!"

"What's he like?" Annie asked eagerly.

Lucy sighed. "Stubborn."

"No, I mean what does he look like?"

"Spectacular—in a high-powered, business-executive kind of way. Why?"

"Because your baby could look like him, of course," Annie explained impatiently.

"Look like him?" Lucy stared blankly at Annie as in her mind's eye an image of a little boy with blue eyes, black hair, and a furious scowl formed. She blinked and the image dissolved, leaving her curiously shaken.

"Excuse me? Could you help me, miss?" A customer approached her and Lucy turned to the woman, glad of the interruption.

Despite her being busy, the afternoon seemed to drag by as the approaching meeting with Andrew refused to be relegated to the back of her mind. And as her apprehension grew, so did her nausea. By the time Andrew arrived to pick her up, she was sorely tempted to call off their dinner engagement and go home and lie down instead. It was only the sure knowledge that sooner or later she was going to have to face him that made her paste a polite smile on her face and follow him out of the shop.

Andrew took her arm, and Lucy tensed as she felt his slightly roughened fingertips brush across her skin. His hand was warm and its heat seemed to seep into her muscles, making her excruciatingly aware of him. She was so absorbed in her uncharacteristic reaction that she allowed him to help her into his car before she remembered that she'd intended to drive her own.

"What's wrong?" He caught her quick frown.

"Nothing, really. It's just that I have my car here. It's parked behind the shop."

"No problem." He pulled away from the curb. "I'll bring you back here afterward. You're perfectly safe with me."

"I'll try to remember that," Lucy said ruefully. She leaned back against the Porsche's soft leather upholstery and tried to relax, but she found it impossible. It was such a bizarre situation. She didn't even know how this man liked his coffee, and she was pregnant with his child.

Blast Miss Day anyway, Lucy thought in frustration. If she'd just had the common courtesy to tell Andrew that she'd changed her mind... Lucy stole a quick glance at him, her eyes lingering on his strong jawline. Maybe it wasn't so surprising that Miss Day had taken the easy way out and simply run. Andrew Killion would be a formidable opponent. But one that she had every intention of beating, she thought grimly. She wasn't some young woman in her early twenties like Miss Day. Not only was she almost fifteen years older, but she was a successful businesswoman well used to dealing with problems. And Andrew Killion certainly constituted a problem. She eyed him consideringly.

"I don't bite. At least not unless specifically invited to." He gave her a quick, infectious grin that Lucy found herself unexpectedly responding to.

"Speaking of biting, why did Miss Day cut and run?" She decided to try to get some information.

"She said she changed her mind," he answered with a promptness that encouraged her to continue probing.

"Why on earth don't you simply get married if you want a child?" Lucy asked the question that had been bothering her from the first.

"Why didn't you?" he countered.

"The available pool of unmarried men in my general age group is growing significantly smaller with each passing year. And, when you add to that the fact that I work in a yarn and needlework shop with an almost exclusively female clientele..." She shrugged. "My chances to meet eligible men are pretty limited. But you would have had a lot more opportunities to marry."

"I tried marriage. It didn't work out." He turned into a parking lot. "I'm not very familiar with the restaurants in Northport, but my secretary assures me that this one is quiet enough that we can talk."

So he'd been married. Lucy was surprised at his words. Recently? Was that why he'd looked for a surrogate instead of a wife? Because he was still hurting over the divorce? Was he still in love with his ex-wife? On the surface it didn't seem likely. Andrew Killion appeared much too self-possessed to ever wallow in unrequited love. But on the other hand, it also seemed highly unlikely that his ex-wife would have divorced him. He appeared to have everything going for him—rugged good looks, money, he was well-known in his field and, if Mr. Marton was to be believed, well respected.

"On the other hand, if you don't like it we can always go somewhere else." Andrew broke into her confused thoughts.

Lucy stared into his clear blue eyes, mesmerized by the tiny lights dancing there. If the poets were right and the eyes really were mirrors of the soul, then Andrew Killion's soul was seething with impatience, she thought ruefully. Not that she blamed him, exactly. He had brought her out to talk, and she kept going off into trances.

"Sorry." Lucy made a determined effort to appear her normal, competent self. "I'm a little distracted tonight."

"You're practically comatose." His smile robbed the words of any sting. "I was saying that if you didn't like my choice of restaurants, we could go somewhere else."

Lucy turned and looked at the yellow brick building. She'd eaten here many times before, and while her floral cotton blouse and skirt were slightly casual, at six it was early enough that it wouldn't matter.

"This is fine," she responded, hoping that the restaurant's elegant atmosphere would help to keep their discussion from disintegrating into an outright fight.

Her first hint that it might not be that easy came when the waitress asked them if they'd like a before-dinner drink. Andrew immediately refused for both of them. Lucy let his high-handedness pass mainly because she intended to have a glass of wine with her meal and she didn't think it would be a good idea to have more than one drink.

Lucy studied the menu longer than she needed to, loathe to abandon such an innocuous subject as food. Finally, she turned to the hovering waitress and said, "I'd like a salad with Roquefort dressing, baked halibut, au gratin potatoes and a glass of white wine."

"Ginger ale," Andrew inserted.

"You want ginger ale, sir?" the waitress asked.

"Not me. Her. She can't have wine. She'll have ginger ale instead." Andrew gave the waitress a charming smile and to Lucy's disgust the woman changed the order without another word.

Lucy clenched her teeth against a furious retort and stared down at the red tablecloth. How dare that...that overgrown male chauvinist pig change her order! And to ginger ale, of all things. She didn't even like ginger ale, for heaven's sake. She seethed in silence until the waitress left and then retorted, "If you ever have the unmitigated gall to do that again, I will get up and leave."

"But, Lucy, you aren't thinking," Andrew defended himself.

"On the contrary, it's because I am thinking that I want to order for myself. How would you know what I like?" she demanded. "You don't know the first thing about me."

"I know you're carrying my child. And I know the results of alcohol on the developing fetus," he said earnestly.

"Excess alcohol," she corrected. "One glass of wine does not constitute excess anything."

"The book on pregnancy my doctor recommended says that no alcohol should be consumed by the mother, just to be on the safe side."

"You've read a book on pregnancy?" Lucy was diverted by the unexpected information.

"Certainly." He looked surprised at the question. "I always research any project."

"I am not one of your projects," Lucy replied emphatically.

"You certainly weren't supposed to be," he grumbled. "If you had just looked at the name on the file you wound up with..."

"And if you had just picked someone a little more mature, she wouldn't have done a flit out the back door," Lucy countered.

"She *was* young," Andrew conceded grudgingly. "But the book did say young was best."

"The book?"

"The one on pregnancy. It says that the late teens are the best time statistically for a woman to produce a healthy baby. The older the woman is, the more prone her offspring is to birth defects. Why, did you realize that at age thirty-five the chances of having a baby with Down's syndrome are phenomenally higher than at twenty?"

"Well, isn't it lucky that you don't have to assume responsibility for my baby, since I've already reached the decrepit age of thirty-five," Lucy snapped.

"I'm sorry. I didn't realize you were thirty-five."

"Being thirty-five is nothing to be sorry about, and anyway, I'll bet you passed thirty-five years ago."

"Yes, but according to the book, the age of the father has no statistically significant correlation to the physical shape of the baby."

"That doesn't surprise me." Lucy gave him a saccharine smile. "I've always known the woman was more important."

"Is that why you've never married?" He eyed her narrowly. "Because you don't like men?"

"I already told you why I haven't married," she answered, having no intention of adding that she was waiting for her ideal man. "And for your information, I do like men. Most men," she qualified with a significant stare at him. "But one doesn't marry for liking. One marries for love."

"True." Andrew winced as if remembering something painful; but before she could figure out a way to probe his reaction, the waitress arrived with their salads.

After the first few bites, it quickly became apparent that the dressing was upsetting her already queasy stomach. Swallowing uneasily, Lucy put her fork down and took a sip of the ice water. Glancing up, she saw Andrew frowning at her, and she rushed into speech to distract him.

"Perhaps we ought to get down to business," she said.

"We already did that!" Andrew's eyes gleamed with unexpected laughter. "That's why we're in this predicament."

Lucy could feel her cheeks burning and it infuriated her. It made her feel less in control of a highly volatile situation.

"This is neither the time nor the place for sexual innuendo," she snapped.

"Sorry." The laugh lines beside his mouth deepened at his patently insincere apology, but she pretended not to notice. She didn't want to notice things about him. All she wanted to do was to get rid of him, she told herself.

"With regard to business," Andrew continued on a suddenly serious note, "as I said before, I was going to pay Miss Day twenty thousand—"

"I was going to pay the sperm donor two hundred and fifty dollars, which should give you some idea of your relative significance in the general scheme of things." She gave him an innocent smile.

He ignored her bit of provocation and went on, "Ten thousand is the going rate for surrogate mothers, but Miss Day had agreed to move into my apartment for the duration of the pregnancy and—"

"And?" Lucy eyed him uneasily.

"And to follow the book's guidelines on health and diet," he finished.

"From what I've already heard about what that book has to say, believe me, you were getting a bargain if Miss Day was willing to go through that for only twenty thousand."

"All right, fifty thousand," Andrew responded with a calmness that was belied by the tiny nerve twitching at the corner of his mouth.

"You could try, but personally your precious, *young* Miss Day doesn't sound like a good risk to me."

"Not her," he said impatiently. "You. Will you take fifty thousand dollars to move into my apartment, follow the book's recommendations and give me my baby when it's born?"

"No. Absolutely, unequivocally no. I will not under any circumstances sell my own flesh and blood," she replied hotly.

"It's my flesh and blood, too," Andrew ground out. "And it's not like you can't have another."

"Ha! According to you, I'm long past the age of having babies. Next year, I'll simply have sunk deeper into my morass of genetic disintegration."

"I think your mind's the first thing to go. You aren't making any sense."

"I'm making a hell of a lot more sense than you are. It takes me nine months to have a child. Your part takes nine seconds. It would make a lot more sense for you to simply start again. You could have your child six weeks after mine."

"Six weeks!" He stared at her incredulously. "Do you have any idea how long it took to find Miss Day?"

"As spacey as she was, I thought you picked her up on a street corner the week before."

"It took eight months from the first advertisement till the psychiatrist said that she knew what she was doing."

"Your psychiatrist is a quack."

"His qualifications are neither here nor there. And we seem to have gotten rather far afield."

"That's because you refuse to accept the simple fact that under no circumstances will I sell my child," she declared vehemently. If they were ever to reach any kind of an agreement, Andrew was going to have to face the fact that he wasn't going to get sole custody.

"You—" Andrew began only to be interrupted by the waitress with their meals.

Lucy ignored his tight-lipped anger, picked up her fork and tentatively poked her halibut. The aroma that reached her nostrils made her stomach lurch protestingly. Under normal circumstances she liked fish, but these weren't normal circumstances. She swallowed uneasily and took another sip of ice water.

Her argument with Andrew was having a devastating effect on her stomach, but she was determined not to let him know. He'd probably only make some crack about her age. She swallowed an uncharacteristic urge to burst into tears. Grimly, she took a bite of the halibut and began to chew, telling herself that it was simply a case of mind over matter.

As a theory, it left a lot to be desired. The longer she sat there under Andrew's angry glare, the more her stomach heaved until finally she put down her fork and concentrated all her willpower on not throwing up.

She was just managing to stay on top of the situation when the waitress served coffee. The aromatic fumes hit Lucy with the force of a blow and she went chalk white.

"Lucy, what's wrong?" Andrew reached for her, but she evaded him. Jumping to her feet, she rushed for the rest room, not caring if everyone was staring at her. They'd stare even more if she lost her dinner on the floor.

To her infinite relief the ladies' room was empty and she was able to throw up in privacy. Finally, when it was all over, she washed her face with cold water, resisting the urge to sit down in the middle of the floor and bawl. What on earth was the matter with her? she wondered in dismay. Her doctor had warned her that she might be feeling a little more temperamental than usual, but this was ridiculous. She felt as if she were on an emotional roller coaster. And Andrew Killion's incessant demands weren't helping any.

She winced as she studied herself in the mirror. She looked exactly the way she felt: colorless and sick, especially sick. If she could just get home without setting her stomach off again ... Concentrate on what comes after the nausea, she told herself. In just a little over seven months, she'd have a baby. A warm smile curved her lips only to fade as she remembered Andrew waiting outside. She might have a baby, but she'd also still have him hanging around her neck like an albatross.

Three

Lucy pushed open the rest-room door and walked out to find Andrew waiting for her. He took her arm and hurried her toward the door, trailed by the very worried-looking manager of the restaurant.

"Is something wrong, madam?" the manager asked "What was it you ate?"

"Oh, that's not the problem." Lucy tried to give him a reassuring smile when she realized what he thought. He was afraid his food had poisoned her.

"You're sure you wouldn't like me to call a doctor?" the man persisted. "You could lie down in my office and wait for him."

"No, she'll do better in her own bed." Andrew put his arm around her shoulder and shepherded her through the door. Grateful for his support, Lucy allowed herself the momentary luxury of leaning against his hard frame; or drawing on his strength to bolster her own depleted reserves.

"But . . ." The man followed them outside.

"The only problem is that she's carrying my child." There was a wealth of primitive satisfaction in Andrew's voice, which not only clashed with his outward air of sophistication but which also made Lucy very uneasy. She didn't want to have to deal with Andrew's feelings. It was hard enough trying to deal with his razor-sharp mind.

"Congratulations!" The manager beamed at them—everything fine, now that he realized his restaurant wasn't responsible for her malaise.

Andrew ignored him as he bundled Lucy into his car. Wearily she stifled a weak desire to cry. It was bad enough that her stomach seemed to have developed a death wish, but now her emotions felt as if they were running wild. And on top of that, she was so tired it was an effort to even buckle her seat belt. She gave a self-pitying sniff.

"Poor angel." Andrew brushed his knuckles over her cheek, and Lucy felt heat flow into her chilled flesh. He leaned over and, pushing aside her fumbling fingers, quickly fastened her seat belt. The warmth of his body momentarily engulfed her as he reached out and gently brushed back a damp curl clinging to her forehead. She could smell the slightly astringent odor of soap on his hands, but there was no accompanying fragrance of cologne. She sniffed again.

"What's wrong?" Andrew moved back into the driver's seat, leaving her feeling curiously bereft.

"Nothing. I was just noticing that you aren't wearing any cologne."

"The book says that pregnant women are very sensitive to odors." He pulled the car out into the swiftly moving traffic.

"If that means that we throw up around perfumes, it's right," Lucy said, strangely touched that he'd alter his normal routine for her comfort. Under a different set of circumstances, she might have liked Andrew Killion very much. But right now, liking him was an indulgence she couldn't afford. She couldn't lose sight of the fact that he wasn't being nice to *her*, he was being nice to her unborn *child*. Not that it was going to do him any good. This was her baby. Other than contributing one cell, he had no claim to it. He wasn't the one who was going to have to endure throwing up in strange bathrooms for months. Men! she thought in disgust.

"Just lean back, close your eyes and relax," Andrew's voice soothed. "We'll be there shortly."

Lucy did, more because it relieved her of the necessity of trying to carry on a conversation than because she thought it would help. She promptly drifted into a drowsy state in which time ceased to have any meaning. Thus it came as a surprise when she opened her eyes and found herself not back at her yarn shop where she'd expected to be, but in front of her own home. She stared at the neat white bungalow as if she'd never seen it before and asked, "How did we get here?"

"I drove," he answered dryly. "Something you're in no shape to be doing." He got out of the car and walked around the Porsche's compact, gleaming hood.

Lucy fumbled with her seat belt, finally managing to free herself just as Andrew opened the door.

"Take it easy." Andrew grasped her elbow as she scrambled out of the car.

"I'm all right," she insisted.

"You're half asleep. You could fall."

"I have an excellent sense of balance," she said, and then promptly tripped over something on the front walk. She would have sprawled flat on her face if Andrew hadn't had hold of her arm. He jerked her backward against him. Lucy could feel the warm thud of his heartbeat echoing in her ear, which was pressed against his chest. It was a strangely seductive sound. She turned her head slightly in negation of the thought, and the finely woven texture of his wool suit jacket brushed against her cheek, further unsettling her.

"What is it they say about tempting fate?" Andrew asked smugly.

"I'm more interested in what I stumbled on." Lucy purposefully stepped out of his encircling arm and looked down at the ground.

"It's a kid's skate." Andrew picked it up. "You're lucky you didn't break your neck."

"It's probably Cindy's." She took it from him and set it on the porch.

"Cindy?"

"Uh-huh." Lucy fumbled in her purse for the key. "She lives next door, and at three she's not much for picking up after herself."

Andrew took the key out of her hand and inserted it in the gleaming brass lock. "By three she should have already learned to pick up her own toys," he stated firmly. "Even the youngest child can be taught neatness."

"Let me guess. Your experience with kids is nil?" Lucy switched on the hall light and stepped inside. To her dismay, Andrew followed her.

"Raising children is simply a matter of common sense," he insisted, ignoring her question. "And being consistent."

"Maybe," she murmured, more concerned with getting rid of him than with listening to his highly impractical theories on child raising.

"Well, thank you for seeing me home." She gave him a bright social smile that faded when he walked past her into her comfortable living room.

"Very nice." He nodded approvingly at the warmth the pale blue and yellow Laura Ashley country print fabrics gave the room.

"I'm glad my decorating meets your approval, but it's late and—"

"And you should be in bed," he finished.

"In bed?" She blinked, her mind suddenly filled with an image of Andrew without the covering cloak of clothes. Was the thick dark hair on his head repeated on his body? Was his chest really as firmly muscled as it had felt when he'd held her so briefly? Stop that, she brought her mind up short, appalled at her unconscious reaction to him. She had to keep sight of the fact that Andrew Killion was her adversary; someone she had to defeat at all costs.

"Yes, in bed." He calmly walked through her small dining room and into the oversize kitchen, with Lucy trailing along behind, wondering what it was going to take to get him to leave. It wasn't that she was afraid of him. She measured his broad shoulders with her eyes. He roused a lot of emotions in her, but fear for her physical safety wasn't one of them. She was as sure as she could be that Andrew Killion would never physically hurt her. But mentally... Now that was something else again. If he were to somehow get what he wanted, he could destroy her emotionally. She closed her eyes against a sudden surge of nausea.

"Bed, right this minute," Andrew repeated firmly as he watched her swallow uneasily.

"It's too early to go to bed," she muttered.

"You don't have to sleep," he coaxed. "Just lie down until your stomach settles. I'll bring you up a cup of something soothing." He turned the heat on under the gleaming brass teakettle sitting on the stove.

"There's some decaffeinated tea in the cabinet on the right, above the stove," she replied, knowing that she shouldn't give in, but unable to resist the unexpectedly pleasant sensation of having someone else take charge for a moment. What harm could it do to let him make her a cup of tea, she told herself. In fact, it would probably help. A cup of tea had always been her mother's panacea for all life's ills. A reminiscent smile curved her lips at the memory. Her mother would have liked Andrew Killion. She had thoroughly abhorred what she had called the tendency of modern men to be wishy-washy. But then her mother had never had to cope with someone like Andrew Killion, Lucy thought ruefully. And certainly not in a situation where so much was at stake. If she had, Lucy was relatively certain that she would have agreed with her daughter that what this situation needed was a little more wishy-washy and a lot less machismo.

"All right," she said. "I'll go lie down, and you make me a cup of tea and after that you can go home, because to be frank I'm simply not up to any more discussions this evening."

"That's obvious. In fact, you barely look up to climbing the stairs." He eyed her speculatively.

"If you're thinking of trying to play Rhett Butler to my Scarlett O'Hara, forget it," she said repressively. "The last thing I need is for you to throw your back out and not be able to leave."

"My back is in perfect shape."

Along with the rest of him, Lucy thought in bemusement as she watched him discard first his suit jacket and then his tie, carelessly tossing them over a kitchen chair. He did have the same black hair on his body, she realized as he folded the cuffs of his white shirt up over his forearms.

"What are you doing?" she finally asked.

"Getting ready to cook," he answered seriously.

"Cook!" Lucy hooted. "You're boiling water."

"I am going to steep tea. It's an art that requires precise concentration." He looked down his nose at her. "And you are going to lie down. Now, if you don't want to be carried, scoot."

Lucy grimaced and headed up the stairs to her bedroom. Since she couldn't physically throw him out, she'd try ignoring him and see if that worked. She flipped on the light as she entered her bedroom so that Andrew wouldn't trip when he brought her the promised cup of tea. She wouldn't put it past him to fake an accident as an excuse to stay. Someone who would try to steal her baby was capable of anything! Her stomach rolled protestingly and she hastily shut down that line of thought.

Kicking off her shoes, she sank onto the bed with a sigh of relief. She felt physically and emotionally exhausted. Lying down, she closed her eyes. She'd just rest for a few minutes until Andrew arrived with her drink.

It was the bright September sunlight which finally woke her. It heated her cheeks and painted an irritating reddish glow behind her closed lids. Confused, she struggled up through the cushioning layers of sleep. There shouldn't be any sunlight. It was night. She prised open her eyelids and found herself staring into a pair of bright blue eyes. Startled, she jerked up only to be promptly pushed back down by a pair of strong hands.

"Don't make any sudden moves," Andrew ordered. "The book says sudden moves'll bring the nausea back."

"Everything brings the nausea back," Lucy grumbled. She peered up at him, realizing that he hadn't spent the night here as she'd first thought. He had to have gone home at some point, because last night's white shirt had been changed for a blue one and he'd obviously had a shave. Her eyes lingered on his jawline. He looked bright, alert and immaculately groomed, while she felt grubby and rumpled in yesterday's clothes and makeup.

"Here." He didn't seem to notice her disgruntled expression.

Lucy automatically accepted the saltines he handed her, frowning uncertainly at them. "Let me guess. You've been cooking again?"

"The book says that eating dry crackers can help control morning sickness. So eat."

He sat down on the bed beside her and Lucy's eyes widened at the feel of his hip pushing against her thigh.

"Eat," he repeated.

Hoping he'd put her momentary confusion down to not being entirely awake, she bit into one of the crackers, trying to ignore the crumbs that were dropping around her neck. She was much less successful at ignoring the heat from his hard thigh, which was seeping into her sleep-relaxed flesh. She was fast becoming aware of him in every fiber of her being. It was not an awareness that she welcomed. This whole situation was volatile enough without her being physically attracted to him.

She gulped down the first dry cracker and started on the second, eager to finish and escape the subtle torture he was unwittingly inflicting on her. And it was unwitting. She shot a quick glance at his face. His expression was distant, as if his thoughts were far away.

As she watched, she saw his lips suddenly firm as if he'd come to a decision. Turning to her, he said, "Since you won't move in with me, I've decided to move in with you for the duration of the pregnancy."

"What!" she yelped.

"I said—"

"I know what you said. What I don't know is why you said it."

He shrugged, and Lucy's eyes were drawn to the way his shoulders strained against the soft blue cotton of his shirt.

"It makes sense to me," he continued. "You have two spare bedrooms across the hall. I can use one of them and you could certainly use someone to look after you."

"No!" Lucy's rejection was all the more emphatic because for one wild moment she'd been tempted to agree—to let him move in; to create the illusion that they were a family. But she knew that was all it would be: an illusion. To Andrew she was nothing more than an incubator for his child. Once her role was completed, he intended to try to grab the baby and run.

"Why not?" he asked reasonably.

"Why not?" she repeated. "I'll tell you why not. In the first place, I don't let strange men move in with me. Or familiar ones, either," she added when he opened his mouth. "In the second, it would serve no purpose because I have no intention of changing my mind. I'm not giving you my baby!" she yelled.

"It's my baby, too." The sadness in his voice cut into her righteous anger as nothing else could have and a deep sense of frustration, fear and guilt churned through her.

Her eyes widened as her stomach reacted negatively to the surfeit of emotion.

"Oh, no," she groaned.

"What's wrong?" Andrew asked sharply.

"Everything," she wailed, and scrambling off the bed, she dashed for the bathroom, making it just in time.

Dimly she could hear water running in the sink as she retched helplessly into the toilet. When it was finally over, she felt a cold, damp washcloth being pressed against her forehead a second before Andrew swung her up into his arms.

"Would you please go away and let me die in peace?" she moaned as he carried her back to the bedroom and gently placed her trembling body on the bed.

"The worst should be over," he said soothingly. "Just rest a few minutes before you get dressed."

"Dressed?" She pushed the washcloth aside and peered up at him. "What time is it?"

He glanced at the wafer-thin watch on his wrist. "Eight fifty-five."

"I don't have time to rest." She handed him the cloth, and determinedly swung her feet over the side of the bed. "I have to get the store opened."

"Let Annie do it."

Lucy's eyes narrowed suspiciously. "How did you know about Annie?" she asked slowly. "She'd already left when you picked me up last night."

"It was in the report."

"What report?" she demanded ominously.

"The detective's report," Andrew admitted warily.

"You had me investigated!"

"Of course I did." He gestured with his hand and Lucy found her gaze caught by the forceful movement. "Look at it from my point of view. I suddenly found out that some unknown woman was pregnant with my child. Isn't it reasonable that I would want to know everything I could about you? Didn't you want to know about me?"

"No!" she snapped. "I just want you to go away before I give in to my first impulse and tear you limb from limb and make my poor baby an orphan!" she heard herself shriek with dismay. What was the matter with her? She rarely lost her temper and even when she did, she never yelled. Never. Yet it seemed as if all she did around Andrew was scream like a fishwife. And even if it was justified, it wasn't productive, she admitted. Screaming at Andrew wasn't going to solve any of their problems. It was simply going to harden both their positions. She took a deep breath and said, "I'm sorry I yelled at you."

Andrew got to his feet and walked to the large window that faced the street, and stared out. The morning sun streaming through, engulfed him in its brilliant glow.

He rubbed the back of his neck, turned around to her and muttered, "For what it's worth, I'm sorry I had that detec-

tive investigate you. How about if we try and start again."
He walked over to the bed and held out his hand. "Good
morning, Lucy. I'm Andrew Killion."

Lucy slowly took his hand, shivering slightly as his callused fingers closed over her much slighter ones. "I'm
pleased to meet you," she responded formally.

"And I you." Andrew stepped back, and Lucy was filled
with an unexpected sense of loss.

She made her voice brisk to cover the fact. "Well, then,
if you'll excuse me, I have to get undressed."

"Oh?" Andrew's eyes began to gleam and Lucy ruth-
lessly suppressed the answering spark of excitement that
sprang to life in her. She absolutely couldn't start to think
of Andrew as the highly potent male he was. That way led
to sure disaster.

"Don't let me stop you." Andrew's husky voice slipped
through her mind.

"I think that's my line," she said crisply. "There's the
door. And in the words of someone or other, don't call us,
we'll call you."

"Yes, but call me what?" Andrew chuckled, although to
Lucy's relief he did leave. She desperately needed some time
away from him. Preferably about twenty-one years.

She got to her feet determined to ignore her unruly stomach. To her surprise, she had no problems. She felt fine. She
felt even better once she'd had a shower. Quickly dressing,
she applied the minimum of makeup and, happily hum-
ming the fourth movement of Beethoven's Ninth Sym-
phony, hurried downstairs.

"Damn!"

She jumped at the sound of Andrew's voice coming from
the kitchen. He hadn't gone home, she realized. He was still
here—she eyed the dish towel tucked into his belt—and
making himself right at home, from the look of things.

"Why 'Damn'? And what are you still doing here?"

"You need a ride to work, remember? You left your car at the shop last night and 'damn' because I can't carry a note in the proverbial bucket."

"So don't sing." Lucy tore her gaze away from the little blue ducks decorating his flat abdomen and walked past him into the kitchen.

"But you can't carry a tune, either," he accused.

"So don't listen." She walked over to the counter to investigate the steam rising from a cup sitting there. It was tea.

"I was thinking of the baby. He's going to be a complete washout musically."

"That doesn't necessarily follow, and anyway, it'll be a chance to test environment versus heredity. I'll start her on violin lessons when she's three."

"He might like to play the trumpet."

"Then she'll just have to learn that life's full of little disappointments. Tell me—" she glanced around the spacious kitchen "—while you were making yourself at home, did you by any chance make any coffee?"

"The book says that coffee aggravates morning sickness, so I made tea."

With a sigh, Lucy picked up the tea and took a sip. She didn't much care for tea first thing in the morning, but at least it was hot.

"Eat your breakfast and then we'll go." Andrew pulled the towel out of his belt and tossed it on the counter.

"Breakfast?" She glanced at the table for the first time. There were several dishes on it, and she moved closer to investigate. There was a small bowl of a white creamy substance dotted with what looked like large brown bugs, a dish of biscuit cereal, a bright yellow banana and a large glass of milk.

She felt a warm glow that Andrew had gone to the trouble to fix her a breakfast, until common sense told her that it wasn't her he wanted to nourish; it was the baby. But that stuff was more likely to poison the poor little thing. She eyed the unappetizing-looking cereal with a jaundiced eye.

"If you'll let me move in with you, I'll fix you breakfast every morning," Andrew bargained.

"Threats will get you nowhere. And after that bout of morning sickness I just had, I have no intention of eating."

"Bad idea. The book says that morning sickness is like seasickness—you have to keep your stomach full. Now eat up and then I'll take you to work."

"Even if I wanted to eat, I don't consider that—" she waved a hand toward the table "—food. And where did it come from, anyway? You certainly didn't find that mess in my refrigerator."

"I brought it with me, and it isn't a mess. Not only is it full of calcium, fiber and vitamins, but there isn't a preservative in the lot."

"Too bad." Lucy smiled. "I could use a little preservation right now."

"Just eat some of the yogurt," Andrew urged.

"Oh, all right." She picked up the bowl of brown-specked yogurt and began to eat it.

"Good, isn't it?" Andrew demanded.

"No," she replied succinctly. "It isn't good. It is, however, edible." She continued eating until she'd finished the last of the concoction. To her relief, her stomach made no attempt to rebel. "You know, Andrew, that book of yours might be right about morning sickness. Remind me to get the name of it from you."

"I'll be glad to give you a copy. I have an extra."

"No. I want the name to make sure I don't accidentally buy it. Any book which claims that this is a proper breakfast is not one I care to read."

"You are the most aggravating . . ."

"Funny, that was my assessment of you." She grinned at his frustrated expression. "Come on, it's getting late. I need to get to work."

"But you haven't finished your breakfast."

"I've already had more than I normally have. I am not a breakfast person."

"No wonder you're throwing up so much."

"You, sir, have a definite way with words. Tell you what, I'll take your banana along for a midmorning snack, but I refuse to have anything to do with any cereal that doesn't come with a prize in the box."

She grabbed her purse, shoved the banana inside and headed toward the door, eager to reach the relative sanctuary of her shop. She needed some time to herself, away from Andrew and all the emotion he so effortlessly stirred up.

"Wow, would you look at that!" Annie's awed whisper caught Lucy's attention and she glanced up from the wool she was pricing.

"At what?" Lucy wiggled her aching shoulders and looked around the busy shop. It was full of Saturday-morning shoppers. "Everything seems normal except for the fact that I'm about to fall asleep on my feet, and it's not even lunchtime yet."

"I hate to be the one to tell you, but that's normal, too. I swear I slept away most of my two pregnancies," Annie claimed. "What I was referring to is the hunk climbing out of that fantastic-looking Porsche."

"Porsche?" Lucy felt a surge of adrenaline push back her mind-numbing tiredness. She hurried over to the large multipaned window that faced the busy street and looked out. As she'd suspected, it was Andrew. When he'd dropped her off at work on Thursday morning, she'd told him she'd call him when she felt up to talking to him. Apparently he'd decided that two days was enough time for her to come to grips with the situation. And he was probably right. She sighed. Their problem wasn't going to go away, no matter how long she stalled.

Lucy studied him intently as he took a cardboard box out of the car. It was the first time she'd seen him out of a suit, and somehow the faded jeans and pale blue knit shirt he was wearing made him seem even more formidable—as if in shedding the uniform of the civilized male, he'd also shed a lot of civilization's restraints.

She watched, fascinated at the way the worn denim hugged his muscular thighs and the thin knit fabric stretched across his broad shoulders. No matter what he was wearing, Andrew Killion was not a man to take lightly. Unconsciously she squared her shoulders.

"Hey, he's coming in here," Annie whispered. "I get to wait on him."

"Down, girl." Lucy grinned at her assistant. "He's here to see me."

"Oh?" Annie eyed her curiously. "How'd you meet him?"

"Fate arranged it. And a capricious fate at that. That, my nosey friend, is the father of the baby I'm carrying."

"Good Lord!" Annie yelped.

"I certainly hope so."

"But..." Annie sputtered.

"Later," Lucy promised. She stepped forward as Andrew entered and glanced around the crowded shop.

"Good morning, Lucy." His eyes automatically focused on her stomach and she felt a wave of irritation. Important as this baby was to her, she was also a person in her own right. The least he could do was give lip service to the fact.

"Good morning, Andrew. I'd like to introduce you to my right-hand person, Mrs. Annie Keaton. Annie, this is Andrew Killion."

"Mrs. Keaton." He gave Annie a warm smile and turned back to Lucy. "I brought you something." He handed her the box, totally ignoring the speculative looks he was getting from Lucy's customers.

"Um, thanks." Lucy grimaced at the amount of interest Andrew was generating. "Come on back to the storeroom." She led him through the shop and closed the door behind them. She most definitely did not need an audience for what he might say.

Curious about what he had brought her, she sat down and opened the box. Inside, she found a package of some kind of oat-bran cereal. Puzzled, she turned it over and read, "'No preservatives, no sodium, no artificial coloring or flavoring.' And undoubtedly no taste," she added. Setting it on her crowded desk, she looked back inside the box and found it filled with the most intriguing collection of junk she'd ever seen. She picked up a handful and discovered a glow-in-the-dark skeleton, a large glass marble and a yellow banana man with bendable legs. What on earth? Digging deeper, she found a beaded necklace, a deck of round cards, a secret decoder ring and a painted paper fan.

"You said you didn't eat cereal that didn't come with a prize, so I provided the prizes."

"From the look of it, you provided the prizes for half of Manhattan." She eyed a black rubber shrunken head incredulously. "Where on earth did you get all this stuff?"

"I designed a building last year for a company that sells trinkets of that sort wholesale. I called them yesterday and asked for a box of samples. Speaking of designing, this room isn't." He looked around.

"Isn't what?" Lucy set the box down on her desk and watched as he poked at the frame of the room's one tiny window.

"Designed. It's also in very bad shape," he said in disgust.

"I know. All the shops on this street were originally houses built in the late 1790s. This room was an add-on in about 1860 and the builder who did the remodeling for me said it was past saving. He suggested ripping it off and putting up a new addition, but I couldn't afford it then. And later, when I could, the timing never seemed right. I intend to tear this down and build on a sort of personal day-care center for the baby."

To her surprise, Andrew didn't immediately claim sole rights to the child. Instead, he looked around again. "Who's your architect?"

"I haven't gotten that far yet. All I've done is ask the builder if he can do it this winter."

"I'll take care of it for you," Andrew muttered, staring up at the sagging ceiling. "We can discuss what the baby will need tonight over dinner."

Lucy opened her mouth to tell him that it was her shop and her addition and she'd make her own plans, when she thought better of the idea—for several reasons. First, his offering to help her with the addition was tacit agreement on his part that he wasn't going to demand sole custody of the baby. Second, if Mr. Marton was to be believed, Andrew was an excellent architect, and she might as well use his services because it was a cinch she had no idea how to go about putting on an addition. But mostly she agreed because of the longing she could see in his eyes—a longing she understood. Much as she regretted the fact, this was his baby, too. Even if she couldn't let him have what he really wanted— sole custody—she could share some of the preparation with him.

"I'd appreciate your help," she said, and was rewarded with a warm smile that sent a surge of pleasure through her.

Four

Lucy pulled into her driveway and turned off her car engine. She closed her eyes, momentarily giving in to the tiredness that had dogged her all day long. She knew that fatigue was a normal part of early pregnancy, but this wasn't her idea of fatigue. This was the deep, bone-weary ache of total exhaustion. All she wanted to do was to crawl into bed and not surface until she had to open the store again Monday morning, but she couldn't. She had promised to have dinner with Andrew. And much as she wanted to cancel, she didn't want to do anything to upset the very delicate accord they'd reached this afternoon. His tacit agreement that he wasn't going to get sole custody had paved the way for her to take Mr. Marton's advice and begin to negotiate what was going to happen once the baby was born.

What did Andrew actually hope to get out of their negotiations? she wondered, absently drumming her fingertips on the Voyager's blue steering wheel. Fathers' rights were a hot legal issue, but not one she'd paid much attention to since it hadn't concerned her. Mr. Marton had mentioned shared custody, but what did that really mean? That the baby would spend a week with her and then a week with Andrew? Even if a judge ignored the emotional trauma that such constant shifting would certainly cause the child, the logistics would be horrendous. And as the child got older, school would be a problem since he or she could hardly alternate schools.

Lucy sighed and slowly climbed out of the car. She was too tired to try to figure it out now. Fishing her back door key out of her purse, she started to insert it in the lock when she suddenly realized that the door was ever so slightly ajar.

She eyed it nervously, trying to remember if she'd closed it when she'd left that morning. Usually she was meticulous about locking the house. The crime rate in Northport wasn't particularly bad—certainly not what it was in New York City, thirty miles to the west, but there was still crime here. And single women living alone were always a target.

Lucy inched closer to the large window beside the door and peered into the kitchen. Her fear was immediately drowned in a flood of righteous indignation. She shoved open the door and stalked inside.

"What are you doing in my house?" she demanded of Andrew.

He turned from whatever it was he was doing at the sink and gave her a sharp, assessing glance.

"Well?" she demanded belligerently.

"Fixing dinner. From the looks of all the customers in your shop this morning, I thought you'd be too tired to go out."

Her minister was right, Lucy thought ruefully. A soft answer did turn away wrath. It also made her feel petty and small-minded.

"I'm sorry I snapped," she muttered. "You're right. I am tired, and I'd much rather eat here than go out. But that still doesn't explain how you got in."

"With the key you gave me. Not that I really needed one. A Cub Scout with an army knife could have forced your kitchen door. Your security leaves a lot to be desired."

"I'll say." Lucy gave him a significant look but he ignored her.

"I'll have a friend of mine put in some real locks for you."

"If you'll give me his name..." she said, of two minds about calling him. She didn't like the way Andrew was becoming involved in her life—first the baby, then her taste in food, then the addition on the shop and now the locks on her house. On the other hand, if her locks were really that bad, maybe she should look into it. She'd never been an advocate of cutting off her nose to spite her face.

"He won't come for you." Andrew stirred something cooking on the stove. "He owns a company that installs the security for the office buildings I design. He normally doesn't do private residences."

"I wouldn't want to put your friend to any trouble."

"You won't. I will. I'll feel much better, knowing you're safe."

No, he'd feel much better knowing his baby was safe, she thought cynically. Andrew Killion couldn't care less if some burglar smacked her over the head and tossed her into the Long Island Sound. All he cared about was that nothing happen to her while she was carrying his baby. After that, she was on her own.

"In that case, I accept," she finally said, deciding that security was more important than independence.

She opened her refrigerator to get a cold drink, frowning as its contents registered. It was full of all kinds of things she would never put there—although, from the looks of some of them, they could simply have developed from moldy leftovers. She studied a plastic container filled with what looked like sprouted grass seed. Pushing aside something labeled Tofu, she took out a can of cola. She opened it, took a long, satisfying swallow and asked, "What's all the junk doing in my refrigerator?"

"Your refrigerator was almost empty." Andrew carefully stirred a small cup of an orangish substance into the frying pan.

"I've heard that nature abhors a vacuum, but this is ridiculous." Lucy sat down at the kitchen table, slipped off her shoes and blissfully wiggled her toes.

"What's ridiculous is how bare it was." Andrew added a container of white stuff to the pan.

"Sunday is my regular shopping day."

"Is that wise?"

"Shopping on Sunday?" She frowned at him, suddenly uneasy. Was he some kind of religious fanatic? He certainly seemed fanatic enough in his attempts to get custody of her baby.

"No. Having only one day off a week. You need more rest than that."

"I can rest anytime I want in the storeroom, except on Mondays and Tuesdays when I'm alone in the shop. What religion are you?" she asked, focusing on her earlier thought.

"What?" He looked startled at her question.

"What religion are you?" she repeated patiently. "It'll be better for the baby if we aren't trying to teach it two opposing philosophies."

"I haven't got a religious philosophy. At least, not precisely." He gestured impotently. "I mean, I'm a Christian, but I don't belong to any formal religion."

"Ah, one of those." She nodded sagely.

"What do you mean, 'One of those'?" he asked defensively.

"A holly-and-lily Christian. The kind you only see in church at Christmas and Easter," she elaborated at his blank look. "Since it can't matter to you, I'll raise my baby in my faith."

"And what religion is it that you're proposing to raise my child in?" he demanded suspiciously.

"I'm a Methodist."

"Methodist?" He squinted off into the distance. "I can live with that."

"Then why haven't you?"

"Haven't I what?"

"Lived with it. Children need the stability of a constant set of values. They should be taken to church, not sent. And I go to church every week, so I ought to have custody on Sundays," she slipped in.

"I can take him to church, too."

"You aren't a member," Lucy pointed out.

"I can join. The requirements aren't high. When last I heard, they were still recruiting sinners," he remarked wryly.

"Well, you'll certainly give them plenty of raw material to work with," she sniped. "Do you have any idea where the nearest Methodist church to you is?"

"No, I'll use yours."

"Mine?" She raised her eyebrows. "That's a long way to come every Sunday."

"Only for a year or so. I own a couple of acres in Oyster Bay I bought years ago to build a house on and then never seemed to find the time. But now that I have a child to consider, I intend to start on the plans just as soon as I finish up my outstanding projects. With any luck at all, it should be done by next fall."

"I see," Lucy said hollowly. She'd been counting on the fact that a judge would be likely to view her home with its big yard as a more suitable environment for a child than some apartment building in New York City. And now Andrew was telling her that he was going to build in Oyster Bay's exclusive enclave; and not just build, but build on acres. It wasn't fair, she thought tiredly. And not only that, but Oyster Bay was just a few minutes away. He'd always be underfoot, trying to interfere.

She swallowed uneasily as her stomach twisted at the thought.

"I think you'd better eat before you get sick again." Andrew eyed her pale face worriedly. "Remember what I told you about keeping your stomach full."

"You've told me lots of things. That's not to say that I believe them. What is for dinner?" She glanced at the food he was putting on the table.

"A spinach and mushroom salad with Dijon mustard dressing, apricot chicken in yogurt, a baked potato, a fresh veggie mixture and a milk pudding dessert."

"I love Dijon mustard," she responded with part of the truth.

Andrew gave her an approving smile that sent a small flare of warmth through her tired body. She found herself smiling back, despite the fact that she loathed chicken, barely tolerated yogurt, and saw absolutely no reason to waste calories on puddings, of all things. Eating his version of a healthy meal seemed a small price to pay for the novel experience of coming home and finding her dinner nearly ready and someone concerned about how tired she was. But she knew it would be a bad idea to allow herself to become accustomed to that luxury. Once the baby was born, her contact with Andrew would be minimal. And that was the way she wanted it, she assured herself. She was an intelligent, competent, mature woman who didn't need to look to anyone else for emotional support. She could provide it for herself. And later, after the baby was born... A soft dreamy smile curved her lips at the thought.

"You look like a medieval Madonna," Andrew murmured.

"There's nothing the least bit old-fashioned about me," she replied prosaically. Picking up her fork, she took a bite of the salad he'd placed in front of her. To her surprise, it was delicious and she gave credit where credit was due.

"This spinach salad is very good. What deli did you buy it from?"

"I made it. Delis tend to use too much salt."

"You made this?" she repeated incredulously.

"The great chefs of the world have always been men," he pronounced smugly.

"I said it was very good, not fantastic. And besides, you're not a great chef, you're an architect. Where did you learn to cook?"

"About five years ago my blood cholesterol topped two hundred, and my doctor suggested I quit living on fast food. Since Amanda was rarely home before eight, I took a couple of courses in cooking that the Heart Association sponsored."

"Amanda?" Lucy latched on to the name.

"My ex-wife. What's your cholesterol level?" He shot the question at her.

"I haven't the foggiest," she answered absently, her mind on what he'd just said. So his ex-wife had worked late every night. Was that why his marriage had broken up? She bit back the questions hovering on her lips. Not only did she have no right to delve into his previous relationships, but she didn't want to, she told herself. The baby was enough of a tie.

"You don't know your cholesterol level! How can any adult in this society not know their cholesterol level?"

"Easy. I have never been a fan of letting people stick needles in me and suck out my blood. It was bad enough when my doctor did it last week to make sure I wasn't anemic." She shuddered as she glanced down at the inside of her elbow. "He kept muttering about chicken veins and stabbing that huge needle in my arm."

"You poor angel." Andrew gently rubbed the still-visible bruise under her skin.

Lucy stared in bemusement at the deeply tanned fingers that stood out in stark relief against her ivory skin tones. Dark against light, she thought dreamily as her body absorbed the soothing feeling of his lightly caressing fingertips. She looked up to find her gaze caught and held by the warmth in his eyes.

"We'll have it done by my doctor," he told her soothingly. "He has a deft hand with a needle."

Lucy opened her mouth to agree and then closed it as she realized what he was doing. He was very effectively using her physical susceptibility to him to get her to agree to do what he wanted. The question was, was he doing it on purpose? Did he realize the effect his casual caress was having on her, or was what he was doing instinctive? She stared consideringly into his bright blue eyes.

"Lucy?" he murmured.

She leaned back, breaking the contact and thus the spell.

"No, we won't," she said flatly. "I have no intention of going within miles of another maniac with a needle."

Prepared to ignore any more arguments, she took another bite of salad. But to her surprise, Andrew, after one frustrated grimace, allowed the subject to drop and the rest of the dinner passed in companionable silence.

"That was delicious." Lucy peered down into the bottom of the pudding cup to see if she'd missed any. "And you could hardly tell the chicken was chicken."

"Thank you?" Andrew questioned dubiously.

"That was a compliment. The reason I can't stand chicken is because it looks like what it was before someone did it in. Your chicken was just a hunk of anonymous meat."

Andrew laughed. "I'll remember that. In the meantime, why don't you go lie down on the living room couch and relax while I clean up the kitchen."

"But you cooked the meal." Her innate sense of fairness made her object, even though lying down sounded heavenly.

"And you worked all day and you're pregnant. Go rest."

About to argue, Lucy decided not to. Andrew was right; she was tired.

"Thanks." She smiled at him. "I really appreciate it."

"Not at all," he said. "After all, it's my child that's making you feel so badly. I feel partially responsible."

"Yes," Lucy muttered, and made her escape, chilled by his reminder of just why he was being so nice to her.

She sank down onto the recliner and leaned back, closing her eyes as if by her action she could shut out all her problems. Almost instantly she was asleep.

Some time later she became aware of a sensation of drifting, of floating. She snuggled her cheek into the hard cushion, frowning at the sound of heavy, rhythmic beating that filled her ear. Vaguely confused, she forced open eyelids that had seemed glued together and found herself staring at a pale blue field that was soft to the touch. She slowly rubbed her palm across the surface, discovering the slightly springy texture beneath.

She tilted her head back and peered upward, straight at Andrew's darkly shadowed jawline. "You must have a very heavy beard," she observed, murmuring her discovery aloud.

"So I've been told." He lifted her higher against his chest as he started up the stairs.

By whom? By women he'd dated? By his ex-wife, she wondered with a flash of some emotion she refused to even acknowledge, let alone explore.

"Where are you carrying me?" She decided to ask a question she had a right to know.

"Up the stairs."

"Maybe I phrased that wrong. *Why* are you carrying me?"

"Because you fell asleep in the chair."

"Do you always carry off women who fall asleep in chairs?" Her voice wobbled slightly as he gently dropped her on her bed.

"I do if they happen to be idiots who are pregnant with my child."

"I am not an idiot." She denied the part she could.

Andrew didn't answer. He merely moved her over slightly and sat down beside her.

Lucy felt her sleep-relaxed muscles begin to tense as his hard thigh pressed against hers. She peered up into his face, looking for some sign that the response was mutual. For all the interest his calm features showed, she could have been a ninety-year-old woman. The realization stiffened her pride as nothing else could and she repeated, "I am not an idiot. And to prove it, I want you to go home. And leave my key behind when you do. I don't like coming home to find strange men in my kitchen."

"Well?" she demanded when he continued to sit, studying her. His scrutiny made her very uncomfortable—as if he could see beneath the surface to her body's involuntary reaction to him.

"Considering the state of your locks, you're liable to come home one day and find most anything in your house."

She grimaced. "Great. Just what I needed. Something for my peace of mind."

"If you'd let me use your spare room you wouldn't have to worry," he slipped in. "I'd be here to protect you."

Yeah, but who's going to protect me from you? Lucy thought ruefully.

"Those new locks your friend's going to install will do that," she countered, watching frustration darken his eyes to slate blue.

"What time is it, anyway?" She glanced at the digital clock beside her bed, her eyes widening in disbelief. "I can't have been asleep for three hours!"

"That store's too much for you," Andrew told her. "When you add the normal tiredness one feels in early pregnancy—"

"Oh? Are you feeling tired?" Lucy asked.

"—to trying to run that blasted shop," he continued doggedly, "you're driving yourself into the ground. Look at you." He gestured toward her, and Lucy's eyes were caught by the reflected glint of gold from his watch. Her eyes focused on his forearm. It was covered with the same dark hair that was on his head. And on his chest; she remembered the springy texture of it against her hand.

"You're so tired, you can't even concentrate on what I'm saying," Andrew remarked in exasperation.

"It's not tiredness I'm suffering from, it's boredom. You sound like a broken record. Besides," she rushed on when he opened his mouth, "as you just pointed out, this tiredness is normal and should fade by the fourth month." Should I live so long, she added on an inward sigh.

"That's two months away. You can't keep up this pace. Let me hire someone to help out in the shop at least on Saturdays and the days when Annie isn't there."

Lucy suppressed her instinctive refusal to allow him even a suggestion about how she ran her shop and forced herself to consider what he was saying. She really was exhausted. Much more so than she'd expected to be by what was in es-

sence a pretty normal Saturday. And her tiredness seeme
to be getting worse, not better. The very thought of tryir
to endure days as bad as this one for two more months ap
palled her. Especially when there was no need for her to tr
to carry on as normal.

"Actually, I'd planned on adding another part-time pe
son in April when the baby is born," she said slowly. "B
it would seem to make good sense to add her now."

"We can get someone on Monday."

"There's no *we* about it. *I* will hire someone, and *I* w
pay her salary." She gave him a level look. "I run a ver
successful business. It doesn't need to be subsidized."

"I wasn't suggesting it did. But since it's my baby, I fe
I should pay—"

"Solomon would have had a tough time with you, n
friend," she stated ruefully.

"All right." He gestured impotently. "No subsidies. B
you will hire someone on Monday?"

"I'll start looking for someone on Monday," Lucy co
rected. "But it isn't going to be easy. I need to find some
one who not only wants to work part-time, but
knowledgeable about at least some aspect of needlework.

"To run a cash register?" Andrew prompted skepticall

"To answer questions. A lot of our customers need hel
with their projects. It isn't going to do me any good to hir
someone who's constantly running to me with questions."

"No, I guess not. But you will start looking on Mo
day?"

"I promise," Lucy said, meaning it. "I have absolutel
no leanings toward masochism."

"How about sadism?" Andrew asked, his eyes full o
lingering sadness.

"Andrew!" Lucy instinctively grabbed his hand, her fir
gers curling around his. "I don't want to hurt you. In fact

rather like you," she admitted. "But what you want can only be bought at the price of my own sanity."

"I know." He cupped her face with his free hand. His callused palm scraped abrasively across her cheek. There was a feeling of security in his touch. A feeling of safety.

"How about if we both stop referring to the baby as 'mine' and try 'ours'?" he suggested.

Lucy took a deep breath and replied, "I'll try. I really will try."

"Good," he said briskly and stood up. "In that case I'll leave you to get some sleep."

Lucy laughed. "I think you could leave me anywhere and I'd get some sleep."

"See that you do. I have to fly to San Francisco tomorrow morning. Remember what I said about keeping your stomach full. I left your refrigerator well stocked."

"Thanks," she acknowledged wryly, planning on tossing it all out first thing in the morning.

"At least try it," he urged. "You liked dinner tonight."

"Yes," she admitted honestly. "The salad and the chicken were quite good. But those alfalfa sprouts tasted like grass and the bean sprouts looked like worms and I still think that puddings are a waste of good calories." She studied him thoughtfully for a few minutes and then suggested, "Why don't we try a compromise? How about if I eat that tasteless cereal you brought for breakfast, and you keep your mouth shut about my choice of desserts?"

"For how long?" he bargained.

"The duration of the pregnancy." It took a real effort for her to make the offer, but her own doctor had said she needed fiber in her diet and she didn't really think there was much fiber in jelly doughnuts, which were her own choice for breakfast.

"It's a deal," Andrew agreed, with a crafty look that made her wonder what he was planning. Knowing him probably brainwashing, she thought ruefully.

"Take care." He dropped a quick kiss on her forehead and she tensed as she felt the warmth of his lips on her skin. "I'll see you when I get back from the Coast."

Lucy bit back an urge to ask him when that would be afraid she might give him the idea that she felt she had the right to monitor his movements.

Almost as if he'd read her mind, he paused in the doorway and added, "If you should need to get in touch with me for any reason, call my office. They'll be able to contact me."

"I'm sure I won't have to bother you." She watched him leave, and then closed her eyes, falling asleep with the ease of a light going out.

As she'd expected, she hadn't needed to get in touch with Andrew. But the fact that she'd wanted to bothered her. She had found herself glancing up when the shop bell rang, half expecting it to be Andrew coming to see how she was doing. Not that he came about her—she mocked that feeling. All Andrew cared about was the baby.

She glanced down at the wallpaper-pattern book she was studying. The tiny, randomly scattered yellow rosebuds on a white background were exactly what she'd pictured in her mind. Now, if she could just locate the exact white canopied crib she wanted...

"Lucy?" Annie hurried into the storeroom. "Do we have any more of that fuchsia silk yarn in a fingering weight?"

"Uh-huh." She pointed to one of the boxes against the far wall. "It's already priced and catalogued. I simply hadn't gotten around to putting it out."

"No wonder." Annie carefully counted out four skeins of the shimmery stuff. "As busy as it was this morning, we haven't had a chance to even think. I swear it's as if the whole island suddenly remembered that it's less than three months to Christmas and they need to get started on their holiday projects.''

''It sure seems that way.'' Lucy ran her fingers through her brown hair. ''But look at the bright side. When the rest of the retailers are run off their feet in December, we'll be relatively quiet.''

''Speaking of being run off your feet, you look like hell,'' Annie said bluntly. ''Things are winding down. Why don't you go on home? We close in a couple of hours anyway.''

''Thanks, but I think I'll stick it out. As you say, it's only another couple of hours.''

''If you say so.'' Annie, clearly unconvinced, picked up the yarn and hurried back to the front of the shop.

Lucy took a deep breath, trying to ignore her queasy stomach. They'd been so busy, she hadn't had time to eat a proper lunch. She'd made do with the hamburger and french fries Annie had brought back for her. It had been a mistake. Her stomach, which had given her almost no trouble during the week Andrew had been gone, was reacting to all that greasy food with a vengeance.

Tiredly she crossed her arms on the desktop and laid her head on them. Perhaps if she emptied her mind of all thought and tried relaxing, it would help. She promptly fell asleep.

Some time later, the sound of someone walking into the storeroom woke her. She raised her head, wincing as her stiff muscles protested.

''This is where I came in.'' Andrew's deep voice sent a shock wave of pleasure through her.

''You're back,'' she muttered disorientedly, staring at him. Deep lines were carved from his nose to his mouth and the brilliant hue of his eyes seemed dimmed as if the energy that normally lit them had been diverted for use elsewhere.

His jawline had a dark shadow on it and his lips were compressed in exasperation as he studied her.

She yawned hugely. "What time is it?"

"Five-forty." He walked over to her and, standing behind her, began to firmly knead her stiff shoulders.

Lucy felt like leaning back against him, but she didn't. Instead, she forced herself to stand and face him.

"I have to help Annie close," she said.

"The shop's empty, and she was counting the cash drawer when I came through." He glanced down at the pattern book Lucy had been sleeping on and frowned. "You should have used some of your yarn as a pillow."

"I didn't intend to fall asleep, and certainly not on one of Tom's pattern books."

"Tom?" Andrew's voice hardened slightly.

"Uh-huh." She yawned again. "He owns the decorating shop about six doors down. I was telling him what kind of paper I wanted for the nursery and he dropped this book by for me to look at."

"Yellow rosebuds!" Andrew exclaimed incredulously.

"Why not?" she asked. "I saw this gorgeous picture of a nursery once that had white furniture, yards of white lace, and that wallpaper."

"You can't use that color scheme for our baby," he protested. "Especially not in either of those two bedrooms across from yours. They face north."

"So?"

"They won't get enough light. The room will be cold. Developing minds need the stimulation of bright, primary colors to develop properly. Something like..." He flipped through the book and stopped at a vividly colored Winnie-the-Pooh print. "Like this," he said in satisfaction. "That will help his mental development."

"You aren't going to turn out to be one of those Yuppie types who go around labeling the furniture in an attempt to

get their kid to read before it's even potty trained, are you?''
she asked suspiciously.

"No, of course not. Forcing a child is counterproduc-
tive, but this—'' He gestured toward the bright paper.

"Is not my choice, and it's my house.''

"We'll discuss this later.'' He backed off at her emphatic
tone. "Right now, I'm starving and you're tired. Let's go
eat.''

"You haven't had dinner yet?''

"No, I came directly here from the airport. We can pick
up a meal on our way home.''

"You're on,'' Lucy agreed happily, cheered that he'd
come to see her the second he'd gotten off the plane.

Five

―――――

You could have had some of that yogurt I brought for dessert instead of this stuff." Andrew dropped the empty ice-cream container into the trash.

Lucy licked the last bit of chocolate from her spoon and said, "I could hit you over the head with something hard, too, but I won't."

"I could get you low-fat frozen yogurt." He refused to give up.

"Could you get me some peace and quiet from this nagging that keeps ringing in my ears?" She placed her empty bowl in the dishwasher, glanced around the kitchen to make sure there were no more dirty dishes and then started the cycle. "If you'll remember correctly, you agreed not to hound me about my choice of desserts."

"I'm sorry." He ran his fingers through his hair, creating an endearingly disheveled look. "But the baby needs proper nutrition.'' Andrew followed her into the living room.

"And she's getting it. I mean, how many nutrients can a being who only weighs a few ounces want? All that's really needed at this stage is a normal diet and a complete lack of medication," she replied, quoting her doctor.

"You don't eat a normal diet," Andrew grumbled.

"Neither do you. I've never even heard of anyone before who puts Tofu in their salad! And if you say 'It's good for you' one more time—'' She glared at him. She was getting sick and tired of his constant disparagement of her diet. It wasn't all that bad. She swallowed uneasily as her stomach lurched in response to her incipient anger.

"What's wrong?" Andrew demanded.

"You're making me sick to my stomach," she accused.

"Me?" Andrew sputtered.

"Yes, you. I bought a book on pregnancy yesterday and my book says that stress really does make nausea worse, and you are stressing me right out of my dinner. And then where will this poor baby be for nutrients?''

Andrew clamped his teeth together, took a deep breath and then released it on a long, slow sigh. "Sorry," he gritted out.

"S'okay." She nodded graciously, sinking down onto the couch as she watched in fascination as he mastered his anger. His eyes gleamed with suppressed emotion, a dull red flush underlay his deep tan, and the bunched muscles along his jawline gave evidence of the effort it was taking. Andrew Killion was not a man who was used to being thwarted even about small things, let alone something he felt was important. Was that what had caused his divorce? Had he taken to giving his wife orders? Had she been some poor, browbeaten soul who'd finally had enough and left? Lucy didn't know; but what she did know was that it was imperative that she stand up to Andrew, because if she didn't, he'd steamroll right over her, telling her all the time it was for her own good. And what was worse, she'd believe it.

"Well, then, if discussing your lamentable diet's off-limits for the moment, how about exercise? What kind of exercise do you normally do?"

"I walk from the house to the car," she said candidly.

"That's not good and not just because of the baby. You'll have a much easier delivery and return to your prepregnancy shape if you're in shape. And it'd be a shame to mess up a shape like yours." His eyes slipped appreciatively over her slender form.

Lucy's stomach lurched again, but this time the stimulus was the hot gleam that briefly flashed in his eyes. She swallowed uneasily, feeling as she'd once done when she'd thought she was stepping onto the floor and found that there was in actuality one more step—disoriented and off balance. Could she have read that look correctly? Did Andrew find her as physically attractive as she found him? It was not a question she felt like facing at the moment. Instead, she decided to focus on the very legitimate point he'd raised.

"You're right," she admitted. "Both my doctor and the book I bought extol the benefits of a regular exercise program." She grimaced. "The problem is that while the mind is willing, the body is weak."

"Hmm." His glance again slipped assessingly over her slim curves. This time impersonally. "Let's see how bad it really is." He held out his hand, his flat palm facing her. "Try to push against my hand."

"Push against it?" she murmured, her eyes focused on the long lifeline that crossed his palm.

"So I can evaluate your muscle tone," he explained. "It'll give me some idea of what we're up against."

"What I'm up against is smug complacency," she grumbled, slowly getting to her feet. "I'll bet you're one of those disgustingly healthy individuals who huff and puff six miles every day."

"I swim three miles every other day and I never huff and puff. Now quit stalling and push."

"Oh, all right." Lucy carefully fitted her flat palm against his. The heat from his skin seeped into her flesh, sending tremors through her. Gamely ignoring her reaction, she gave a tentative push. Nothing happened. She pushed harder. Still nothing happened.

Lucy glanced up in time to see Andrew's hastily suppressed grin. It was all the goad her pride needed. She couldn't be that out of shape.

She threw the full force of her weight behind her effort this time. It was like pushing on a brick wall. Determined to wipe that grin off his face, Lucy decided that what was needed was a bit of guile. She let up on the pressure she'd been exerting as if she were about to give up, then suddenly stepped on his foot at the same time she lunged forward. The result was not what she expected.

Instead of simply dropping his arm, Andrew jerked back in surprise, caught his calf against the side of the coffee table and fell backward.

Lucy, already off balance, went down with him in a tangle of arms and legs. Her cheek was pressed against the soft cotton of his shirt, and the heavy thudding of his heartbeat echoed through her mind. She shifted slightly as his belt buckle bit into her rib cage and her nylon-clad thigh rubbed tantalizingly over the finely woven texture of his wool pants.

Her own heart began to race as she could feel his instinctive reaction to having her sprawled across his body. Lucy raised her head and stared down into his eyes, fascinated by the tiny silvery lights exploding in them.

"I moved you," she blurted out.

He chuckled, making her gasp as his body shifted beneath her.

"Lucy, you not only move me, you drive me up the wall. You are all right, aren't you?"

She was fine, she acknowledged ruefully. If you discounted the fact that she was fast losing her sense of perspective over the one man in the world that she had to keep at arm's length. Because if she didn't, they'd never be able to reach an agreement about how to handle the custody of their child.

"Lucy?" He gently rubbed her back and she had to resist an impulse to arch into his casual caress. And it was casual, she admitted with her normal lack of self-deception. Andrew's body might react instinctively to having a woman fling herself on top of him, but his mind didn't appear to be similarly involved.

"I'm fine." She scrambled to her feet. "In fact, I should be asking you that question. You're the one who got made a pancake of."

"You can make a pancake of me anytime," he gave her a lighthearted leer and then spoiled it by adding, "but all this proves my point: you're completely out of shape. You'll have to start from scratch."

"I wish I could scratch the whole idea," she said glumly.

"You have to get in shape," Andrew repeated doggedly.

Lucy sighed. "I've already conceded that. I guess I'll call a few of the health spas in the area and ask about aerobics classes for expectant mothers."

"Bad idea." He sat down on her couch, picked up the remote control and turned on the television set.

"Bad idea?" Lucy echoed in confusion. "Just a second ago you were the one touting exercise."

"The right kind. The book says that there are a lot of exercises a pregnant woman shouldn't do, and it warns that even classes specifically advertised for the pregnant woman can be harmful because there are unscrupulous health clubs that don't check out their instructors' qualifications."

"Tell me, did this fount of all wisdom tell you how to evaluate a particular program?" she snapped, heartily sick of hearing about his blasted book.

"Unfortunately no, and that being so, we'll do as it suggests and try walking."

"Walking is boring," she objected.

"Well, how about swimming?" he countered with a promptness that made her feel ashamed of her obstructiveness. "I swim at the health club in my office building in the city, but we ought to be able to find a pool around here. Of course," he added reflectively as he fine-tuned the television set, "there's the problem of having to fit your swimming into the pool's schedule."

"I've got a bigger problem than that," she admitted sheepishly. "I can't swim."

"You can't swim!" Andrew looked at her in shock. "How the hell can anyone have reached the age of thirty-five without being able to swim?"

"It's a natural talent. I guess it'll just have to be walking, after all."

"It's probably just as well." He went back to fiddling with the remote control. "The book says that due to certain changes in a woman's body during pregnancy, they're more susceptible to vaginal infections caused by germs in pools."

"Tell me, does this precious book of yours include a section on first aid?"

"Sure. Why?"

"I just want to make sure you're covered when I smack you one alongside the head."

"Why are you mad?" He looked confused.

"Because..." She struggled to express her annoyance in a way that didn't make her sound like a petulant child. "Because I don't like my body parts being discussed as if they were a separate entity," she finally said. "Is that understood?"

"No, I don't understand at all. But I also don't want to upset you. We'll discuss it later."

At the rate they were accumulating things to be discussed later, they were going to spend the whole ninth months just arguing, Lucy thought with a flash of humor. "Perhaps we could..." She paused as she realized what was on the television screen. "Why are you tuning in that inane game show?"

"Because in one minute, what I want to see will be on."

"Oh? What's that?"

"L.S.U. versus Florida State."

"L.S.U. versus... You mean a football game?"

"That's right. It should be a great game."

"There is no such thing as a great football game. Why, do you realize that if those guys did to each other on a street corner what they do in a game, they'd find themselves hauled up before a judge on charges of aggravated assault?"

"Nonsense," he scoffed. "According to the paper, Florida State is a three-point favorite."

"Give me one good reason why I should let you pollute my living room with that organized mayhem which masquerades as a sport."

"Because you're much too kindhearted to throw my tired body out into the cold?" He gave her a hopeful look.

"In the first place, it's a gorgeous Indian-summer evening and in the second, it isn't kindhearted you're talking about, it's softheaded, which I am not."

"All right. Suppose you let me watch it because our son is going to want to learn how to play football, and apparently I'm going to be the only one able to teach him."

"No son of mine is going to play football!"

"All boys play football. I did."

"Yeah, and look how you turned out," she sniped.

"Thank you. I'm rather pleased with the results, too."

Lucy felt a reluctant smile curve her lips at his smugly satisfied expression. Not wanting to encourage him, she pressed her lips together and stared at the wall behind his head.

"What are you doing?" he asked curiously.

"Counting to ten and reminding myself that it might be a girl."

"Is it important to you that it be a girl?"

"No, but I thought it would probably be easier to raise a girl on my own. As you've just pointed out, I don't know much about boy-type things."

"But you aren't on your own anymore," Andrew replied softly, holding out his hand.

Lucy stared at it a minute, her eyes lingering on his square-cut, immaculately clean nails. "No," she finally admitted, tentatively placing her hand in his. His fingers closed around hers possessively, giving her the feeling that she'd done a whole lot more than just agree with him.

"And that being so, why don't you at least watch the game before you make any rash judgments?" Andrew suggested.

"All right, you can watch the game on my television set, but you'll have to make yourself useful while you're doing it. I'll be right back." She went to get the sack of yarn she'd brought home from the shop earlier in the week.

Sitting down beside him, she dumped the bag's contents into her lap and said, "I need you to hold up your hands about eight inches apart."

Andrew picked up one of the skeins of yarn that had fallen on the floor and rubbed his hand over it.

Lucy watched his sensuously moving fingers, wondering what it would feel like if those fingers were moving across her skin, stroking her bare...

"Very nice," Andrew remarked appreciatively. "What is it? Cashmere?"

She broke free of her fantasy with an effort. "It's alpaca. I had a bunch of odd dye lots left over so I thought I'd make myself a warm, oversize sweater to wear this winter."

"It's certainly warm," he agreed. "I take it my role in this is to hold the skein over my hands while you wrap it into balls?"

"If you would." Lucy dropped the heavy yarn around his hands and began to wind, glancing up at the screen every once in a while when the crowd started screaming. She didn't change her mind. As far as she could see, football was downright dangerous, and no son of hers was going to risk life and limb in its pursuit—no matter what his father was misguided enough to think.

By halftime she'd had more than enough of the game, but she was oddly reluctant to send Andrew home to watch it on his own set. It was pleasant having him here on the couch beside her. More than pleasant; it fulfilled a deep need she hadn't even realized existed—that of companionship. She was lonely, she realized with a distinct shock. Her days might be filled to overflowing with activity, but there was virtually no sharing on a personal level in her life. There was no real companionship with someone she cared about.

This unexpected and totally unwelcome bit of self-knowledge made her restless, and she got to her feet.

"How about a snack?" she asked.

Andrew glanced up from the television set, shook his head as if to clear it and said, "Sounds good to me. How about some of that Tofu cheesecake I got at the deli? It's on the top shelf of your refrigerator. In the back."

"Tofu cheesecake!" Lucy repeated in horror. "Is nothing sacred?"

"Certainly not saturated fat. Want some help?"

"No, it won't take a second." She refused his offer, feeling an inexplicable need to distance herself from him—both mentally and physically.

Ten minutes later Lucy returned to the living room with a tray containing a pot of hot tea, a plateful of chocolate-chunk brownies with thick fudge frosting and a slice of the despised Tofu cheesecake, only to find Andrew sound asleep.

A tender smile curved her lips as she studied his sleep-relaxed features. He looked so peaceful. He also looked younger—not at all like the self-assured man who'd embroiled her in this whole mess.

She set the tray down on the coffee table and sat down beside him, trying to decide what she should do. Waking him up seemed the most logical course of action, but she hated to do it. He seemed so tired. Heaven only knew what kind of schedule he'd been keeping in San Francisco. Probably working all hours of the day and night. And when you added to that the time difference between the two coasts...

She wouldn't wake him immediately, Lucy decided. She'd let him sleep until the end of the ball game. She poured herself a cup of tea and, suddenly ravenous, picked up the biggest brownie.

Two cups of tea and three brownies later, she checked the action on the screen—the players were still beating on each other—and then looked at Andrew. He was still asleep. She yawned; just looking at him made her sleepy. She squinted at the clock on the VCR—nine-fifteen. It was much too early to go to bed. She'd just rest her eyes a minute and then she'd feel better. There was no danger of her falling asleep with the television blaring a constant commentary on the progress or lack thereof of the game.

Her first intimation that she'd been wrong came hours later when the warm pillow she was snuggled up against moved.

"Hmmf," Lucy muttered protestingly and tried to show it into a more comfortable shape, only to find her hand caught and held.

Groggily she opened her eyes and then promptly closed them again when she discovered a pair of blue eyes two inches away.

Andrew! Memory came rushing back, banishing sleep. Unfortunately, along with memory came sensation. She was lying on the couch beside Andrew and could feel his lean body along the entire length of hers; could feel his hard muscles pushing against her much softer ones. Lucy took a deep, steadying breath that pushed her breasts into his chest. Tiny pinpricks of excitement danced over their sensitive surface, and she scrambled for some kind of control over her wayward senses.

Andrew raised his arms above his head and stretched, causing his muscles to ripple against hers.

"The game appears to be over," his sleep-roughened voice observed.

Lucy peered at the TV set and saw a gorgeous blonde almost wearing a skintight dress screaming her head off.

"Not necessarily. They could simply be panning the crowd."

"Philistine," Andrew grumbled. "You have no appreciation for the finer things of life." Getting to his feet, he stretched again.

Lucy watched in fascination as his movement tautened the gray fabric of his pants across his abdomen, making her vividly aware of his masculinity.

He ran his fingers through his thick hair and Lucy's eyes narrowed at the gesture, which made her curious about the texture of his hair. Was it as silky as it looked? Was it—

"—bed." The last word of Andrew's sentence finally got her attention, and she blinked in bemusement.

"What?"

"I said it's time we were in bed. It's two-fifteen in the morning."

"Oh." She thought about that fact a moment and found it uninteresting beside her continued perusal of his magnificent body.

"You need your rest, and I have a long drive home." Lucy's ready sense of sympathy was stirred until he added, "If you'd just let me use one of your spare bedrooms for the duration of your pregnancy..."

And spend the rest of my life remembering what it was like to live with him, she realized on a flash of insight. The depressing thought made her voice sharp.

"I told you once before, it isn't cold out there. It's a gorgeous autumn night and, besides, if you don't want to drive, take the Long Island Railroad."

"Do you know when they run at this hour, or even if they do?"

"That's not my department." She hardened her heart against his pathetic expression, knowing that it had been assumed for her benefit. There was nothing the least bit pathetic about Andrew Killion. "Go home," she told him.

He heaved a gigantic sigh. "Well, if you're determined to cast me out into the cold, cruel world, I guess I have no choice. Come lock the door behind me."

He reached out and Lucy grasped his warm hand, allowing him to gently pull her to her feet. She froze as her stomach lurched in protest at her movement.

"What's wrong?" he demanded sharply.

"Nothing, I guess." She started toward the door when nothing else happened.

"But..." Andrew hurried after her.

"It was just for a minute there I thought my stomach was about to take violent exception to the brownies."

"Brownies?"

"It's all your fault, anyway. If you hadn't fallen asleep I never would have eaten yours, too." She pulled open the door, shivering slightly as the chill air attacked her. It really was kind of cold out there, she thought guiltily.

He chuckled. "I can see I'm grievously at fault." He paused in the doorway and stared down into her face with an expression she found hard to read. Mischief, desire, amusement—they all seemed to be mixed up together, along with other, more elusive emotions she couldn't put a name to.

He reached out and cupped her chin, holding it lightly. "Since it appears I've already blotted my copybook, I might as well be hung for a sheep as a lamb."

"Never mix metaphors," Lucy muttered distractedly, watching as his eyes came closer until they seemed to fill her whole field of vision.

She waited with a feeling of breathless anticipation until his lips finally brushed hers. They were warm—warm and firm as they rubbed against her mouth. Lucy shivered, wanting more than this insubstantial caress. She wanted to explore the taste and feel of those lips. But her desire was left unfulfilled as Andrew raised his head and, with a final gentle kiss on the tip of her nose, left.

Lucy automatically locked the door behind him, her mind still focused on his kiss. Why had he done it? She worried the question around in her mind as she prepared for bed. Simply because he found her physically attractive? She certainly found him attractive enough. She shook her head, trying to dislodge the memory of the feel of his body pressed against hers. He probably didn't have a reason, she finally decided. He'd probably just given in to the impulse of the moment and kissed her. It was nothing to get worked up about.

But strangely enough, the undoubtable truth of her logic didn't make her feel any better and she climbed into bed, out of sorts with both herself and her world, even though she wasn't sure why she felt that way.

Her heavy sleep was finally broken by her subconscious replaying of that disturbing kiss. Slowly, as if her mind were having trouble recalling it, the details started to surface. She could feel the feather-light touch of fingertips brushing her hair back from her temple. Then the fingers moved in a slow, meandering path down her cheek, leaving a shivery sensation behind. She shifted restlessly as the skin on her face seemed to tighten in anticipation. At last, she felt the remembered warmth of Andrew's lips brushing hers and she gave a small sigh of pleasure.

As if her inarticulate sound were a signal, his mouth pressed harder, and the tip of his tongue traced over her bottom lip. Lucy reached blindly upward to find the warm wall of his chest.

Chest? The information filtered down through her sleep-fogged mind. Dreams didn't have chests! Her eyes flew open to find herself staring into Andrew Killion's brilliant blue eyes.

"You went home," she muttered in confusion.

"And I came back." He sat down on the bed beside her. His action tightened the bedding covering her chest, and the material dragged across the sensitive tips of her breasts, making them contract into tight buds.

Ignoring her involuntary reaction, Lucy scrambled to get control of the situation. Father of her baby or not, he had to stop wandering in and out of her bedroom!

"How did you get in?" she demanded. "I distinctly remember locking up after you last night."

"I have a key, remember?"

"That's right. My key. The one I asked you to leave.
Hand it over." She started to hold out her hand, then realized just how poorly her lace nightie covered her since her
breasts had grown, and instead nodded toward the cherry
table beside the bed. "Put it there."

"But—"

She shook her head, and her brown hair brushed against
her sleep-flushed cheeks. "No buts. It's my key and I want
it. Now."

"I really ought to keep your spare," he argued. "What
would happen if you locked yourself out?"

"Having lived here eight years and never having done so,
it's highly unlikely. But on the off chance I did, I'd simply
go over to the shop and get the spare key I keep there. Now
give."

"Okay. Don't get upset." He placed the key on the table.
"Remember your nausea."

She moved experimentally. "I don't feel sick this morning."

"It's because you were woken with a kiss," he said
smugly.

Lucy laughed. "You do appear to work better than dry
crackers."

"You wouldn't like to try for a cure, would you?" The
darkened pupils of his eyes seemed to grow larger under her
fascinated gaze.

"No, I'd like to get dressed. In private," she added when
he made no move to leave.

"Wear something loose fitting. We're going to take your
walk right after breakfast."

"You aren't wearing something loose fitting," she observed, frowning as she noticed that he was wearing a suit—
another one of those gray sartorial creations that she was
willing to bet never came off-the-rack. This time it was

matched with a pale blue oxford-cloth button-down shirt
and a silver-and-navy striped tie.

"I have to catch a flight back to San Francisco after your
walk and there won't be time for me to go home and change.
If you'd just let me at least keep some clothes here—"

"No!" She shook her head emphatically, as much in negation of her feeling of disappointment that he was leaving
again as against what he was asking. "You undoubtedly
belong to the give'em-an-inch-and-they'll-take-a-mile
fraternity. Besides," she went on when he opened his
mouth, "you don't need to move in. You're always underfoot anyway. Now, scat, so I can get dressed."

"I'll get breakfast ready." He started toward the door.
"Would you like a banana in your cereal?"

"No, throw in some of those raspberries in the refrigerator. I'll be down in a minute."

But despite her intention of hurrying, she couldn't seem
to get herself moving. Her mind kept dwelling on the kisses
they'd shared. They were a distinct departure from their
previous exchanges. Could they represent some strategy on
his part? Could he be trying to soften her up by using his
potent masculinity as a weapon?

But toward what end? she wondered. Andrew Killion
wasn't stupid. Far from it. He had to realize that she
couldn't be so easily manipulated. Which brought her back
full circle. Why kiss her? Unless... She thoughtfully yanked
a yellow cable-knit sweater over her head. If there were no
child between them, then she would have no trouble understanding his actions. He was a healthy, attractive man who
desired her—at least in some measure.

Lucy tossed her hairbrush on her dresser, telling herself
not to worry about it. Nothing was straightforward in this
situation. Why should his motives be?

But that was no reason for her not to enjoy his kisses, she told herself. As long as she remembered who and what he was, she wouldn't be hurt.

With a feeling of anticipation that had nothing to do with the thought of exercise, she hurried downstairs.

Six

Finished?'' Andrew asked indulgently.

Lucy glanced in resignation at the small pool of pink-tinged milk in the bottom of her cereal bowl. It appeared she couldn't delay the evil moment any longer. She was going to have to exercise. Stifling a sigh, she put down her spoon and got to her feet. Exercise was good for the baby, she reminded herself, prodding her reluctant will.

''We'll do some stretching exercises first,'' Andrew said.

''What do you mean, we? I agreed to walk—not stretch. Besides, I don't need to practice stretching. I seem to be doing that naturally.'' She tugged at the too-tight waistband of her jeans.

Andrew frowned. ''I told you to wear loose-fitting clothes.''

''I don't have any. What I don't understand is how I could have lost five pounds and gained over an inch around my waist.''

"You'll gain the weight back again soon enough," Andrew consoled her. "But regardless of the fit of your clothing, if you don't stretch before exercising, you're liable to pull a muscle."

"There's no risk of that happening, because I have no intention of moving beyond an easy stroll."

"To begin with," Andrew agreed. "But to get the most benefit for your cardiovascular system you have to raise your heartbeat."

"What's being raised is my blood pressure," she corrected, and was immediately ashamed of the querulous note she heard in her voice.

"I'm sorry," she apologized. "It's not fair to take my dislike of exercising out on you. Especially when I know you're right about it."

"Not to worry." Andrew gave her a warm smile. "It's not your fault. The book says that emotional mood swings are very common during pregnancy, especially early on."

"You know, Andrew, up until you brought that book into my life I'd always been against censorship. But now—" her eyes gleamed "—now, what I'd really like to see is a good old-fashioned book burning."

"Sacrificed no doubt on the altar of stupidity?"

"I was thinking more along the lines of ignorance is bliss," she shot back.

"My poor angel." Andrew reached out and ran his knuckles over her cheek. The fine hairs on her skin seemed to electrify, and she ducked her head to break the unsettling contact.

"This pregnancy hasn't had much bliss in it for you so far, has it?" His gentle voice made her want to fling herself against his chest and burst into self-pitying sobs. And that confused her further. She was not the kind of person who leaned on others, either mentally or physically.

"There's less than seven months to go," she said, "and then I get the baby. And that was my goal—not being pregnant."

"Yes, the baby." A shadow darkened Andrew's face for a moment and then it was gone, leaving Lucy to wonder if he were remembering that the child wasn't going to be his alone as he'd planned. Or hers as she'd planned, she thought. But somehow, that knowledge no longer brought such a sharp stab of anger and fear. While she would still prefer to have the baby all to herself, if she did have to share it with someone, then Andrew was a good choice. Actually, he was an excellent choice, she amended honestly. He was well educated, financially responsible, kind and intelligent—if you discounted his fascination with that blasted book of his.

"What are you looking so fierce about?" he asked.

"I was just wondering whether or not you have a book on how to raise babies. But I give you fair warning, Andrew Killion, if you try to regiment our child's life..."

"Children like a routine," Andrew defended himself. "And bright, primary colors. And quit trying to sidetrack me. You're supposed to be stretching."

"How?" Lucy asked.

"Like this." He turned and, pressing his hands flat against the wall, leaned on them. "Push on your hands," he ordered.

Lucy watched him, her eyes skimming down past his narrow hips and strongly muscled thighs encased in the smooth gray wool of his suit pants to land on his white running shoes. It was an incongruous combination that should have looked ridiculous, but on Andrew it didn't.

"Come on," he urged. "I have a plane to catch in a few hours and I want to show you how to get started so that you can build up your stamina while I'm away."

"How long will you be gone this time?" Lucy asked as she obediently leaned up against the wall beside him.

"Till the weekend, unless something else goes wrong."

"I take it you expect it to?" she questioned sympathetically.

"I don't expect anything from this project. But if I believed in curses . . ." He grimaced.

"I have a customer who's a witch. The next time she comes in I'll ask her for a charm."

Andrew looked at her in disbelief. "A witch who knits?"

"Well, what do you think witches do all the time? Boil things in caldrons?"

"I never thought about it. Mainly because I don't believe in witches. Tell me, does she also read the future in tea leaves?"

"Of course not." Lucy looked down her nose at him. "She uses tarot cards."

"Do you actually believe that junk?" he asked incredulously.

"No, but I'm keeping an open mind," she said. "You must admit there's a lot in this world that is inexplicable."

"Beginning with your thought processes."

"An open mind is a virtue," she defended primly.

"There is a difference between open and vacant," Andrew pointed out. "Besides, you're the one who claims to be a staunch Methodist. How do you reconcile witchcraft with Christianity?"

"How do you reconcile your Christianity with your idolatrous worship of that book you keep quoting?" She grinned, inordinately pleased to have gotten in the last word.

A last word Andrew seemed content to let her have. For, other than a grimace, he ignored the subject, concentrating instead on the exercises they were doing.

"That's enough pushing on the wall," he announced. "Now, try this one." He bent his leg at the knee, grabbed his

NO COST! NO OBLIGATION TO BUY!
NO PURCHASE NECESSARY!

PLAY "LUCKY 7"
AND GET AS MANY AS SIX FREE GIFTS...

HOW TO PLAY:

1. With a coin, carefully scratch off the silver box at the right. This makes you eligible to receive one or more free books, and possibly other gifts, depending on what is revealed beneath the scratch-off area.

2. You'll receive brand-new Silhouette Desire® novels. When you return this card, we'll send you the books and gifts you qualify for *absolutely free!*

3. If we don't hear from you, every month we'll send you 6 additional novels to read and enjoy. You can return them and owe nothing but if you decide to keep them, you'll pay only $2.24* per book, a savings of 26¢ each off the cover price! And there's **no** extra charge for postage and handling. There are no hidden extras.

4. When you join the Silhouette Reader Service™, you'll get our monthly newsletter, as well as additional free gifts from time to time, just for being a member.

5. You must be completely satisfied. You may cancel at any time simply by sending us a note or a shipping statement marked "cancel" or returning any shipment to us at our cost.

*Terms and prices subject to change.
Sales tax applicable in NY and Iowa.
© 1990 HARLEQUIN ENTERPRISES LIMITED

You'll love your elegant 20k gold electroplated chain! The necklace is finely crafted with 160 double-soldered links and is electroplate finished in genuine 20k gold. And it's yours free as added thanks for giving our Reader Service a try!

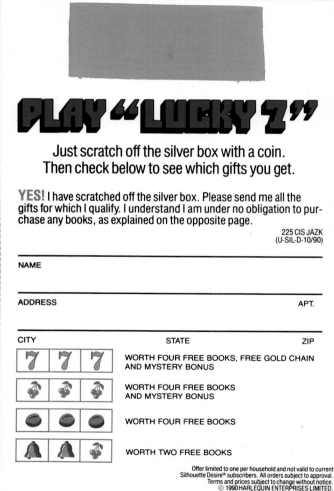

PLAY "LUCKY 7"

Just scratch off the silver box with a coin.
Then check below to see which gifts you get.

YES! I have scratched off the silver box. Please send me all the gifts for which I qualify. I understand I am under no obligation to purchase any books, as explained on the opposite page.

225 CIS JAZK
(U-SIL-D-10/90)

NAME

ADDRESS   APT.

CITY   STATE   ZIP

7	7	7	WORTH FOUR FREE BOOKS, FREE GOLD CHAIN AND MYSTERY BONUS
🍒	🍒	🍒	WORTH FOUR FREE BOOKS AND MYSTERY BONUS
⬤	⬤	⬤	WORTH FOUR FREE BOOKS
🔔	🔔	🍒	WORTH TWO FREE BOOKS

BUSINESS REPLY CARD

First Class   Permit No. 717   Buffalo, NY

Postage will be paid by addressee

SILHOUETTE
READER SERVICE
901 FUHRMANN BLVD
PO BOX 1867
BUFFALO NY 14240-9952

NO POSTAGE
NECESSARY
IF MAILED
IN THE
UNITED STATES

foot from behind and pulled his calf up against the back of his thigh. "Now you try," he ordered.

Gamely Lucy followed his example. At least, she tried. It wasn't as easy as it looked. Determined not to admit she couldn't perform a simple stretching exercise as well as he did, she yanked her foot closer to her body and was immediately engulfed in a red haze of pain.

She dropped her foot and staggered to the kitchen counter, whimpering pitifully.

"Lucy! What's wrong?" Andrew reached for her and then dropped his hands as if afraid to touch her.

Lucy froze, trying to find some relief from the pain that was ripping through her.

"Lucy! What hurts?" He sounded frantic.

"My calf. It's cramping."

"Thank God." His words came out like the answer to a prayer. "For a second there I thought you'd really hurt something."

"Believe me, this *really* hurts," she gritted out.

"No, I meant something like a hamstring pull. Sit down." he gently pushed her down on the floor and, kneeling beside her, took her cramping calf in his hands.

Lucy gasped as he began to massage her tortured muscles. "Don't!" She ineffectively tried to push him away.

"Flex your toes toward your body," he told her, ignoring her command.

Lucy did. And to her surprise, the intense pain immediately began to abate.

"It's working." She collapsed back against the kitchen cabinet in relief.

"Good." Andrew continued his gentle kneading of her calf. "That preventative was recommended by my book." He gave her a significant stare.

"Which just goes to prove that it really is true. There's a spark of goodness in everything," she riposted.

"Or a spark of intelligence, no matter how willfully blind they are?" he countered as his fingers continued their insidious magic.

Lucy ignored his words, preferring to focus instead on the feel of his hands.

The early-morning sun coming in through the bay window spilled over him, drenching him in sparkling light. It lent a golden patina to his tanned skin and added a diamond sparkle to his gleaming eyes.

She reached out to touch the spot where one errant sunbeam was caressing his face. She traced it around the outer whorl of his ear and then down across his jawline, savoring the shivery feeling caused by the rough-silk texture of his skin scraping against her fingertips.

Andrew's hand stilled, and he turned his head toward her. Lucy looked into his eyes, focusing on the tiny silvery lights radiating out from the darker center. As she watched, the pupils expanded under the force of his burgeoning emotions.

"You have the most gorgeous eyes," she said dreamily. "Maybe I'll get lucky and the baby will have them."

"And your adorable little nose—" he ran his fingertip down its bridge "—with that small scattering of freckles."

"I don't have freckles," she automatically protested as she savored his words. Did he really like the shape of her nose or was he just being polite? He liked it, she decided with a feeling of pleasure that vaguely worried her. Andrew Killion was never merely polite.

"And your hair." His voice deepened and Lucy shivered with sudden excitement. "In the sunlight all the fiery little strands of red are visible." He threaded his fingers through it and gently tugged her toward him.

Electricity seemed to dance over her skin, sensitizing it to his touch if not to the dangers inherent in that touch. Her eyes focused on his firm lips with a fascination totally divorced from rational thought. She watched them come closer with a growing excitement that was clearly visible in her eyes.

As his lips met hers, her heartbeat stopped and then lurched into a slow, heavy rhythm that echoed in her mind, drowning out the voice of reason.

Andrew's large hand cupped the back of her head, holding it immobile as he exerted pressure. Her lips parted beneath that pressure, and she felt the heated warmth of his tongue surge inside.

Lucy gasped as pleasure exploded in her mind—pleasure on a scale that she'd never known. It was the very intensity of her response that gave her the strength to withdraw. She was reacting much too strongly. She needed to back off and try to regain some measure of perspective.

Sensing her withdrawal, Andrew raised his head and gave her such a tender smile that she wanted to cry—to cry for what might have been, but wasn't.

"Your leg will feel better once you walk on it a little." Effortlessly he lifted her to her feet and steadied her against his body for a moment while she regained her balance.

"It would probably feel a whole lot better if I didn't walk at all today and rested it instead," she offered without much hope he'd buy her reasoning. He didn't.

"Don't be chicken. You have to work through the pain." He opened her kitchen door and motioned her outside.

"You'd make a great mailman," she grumbled. "Nothing slows you down."

"I don't like those cramps, though," he mused.

"*You* don't like them? How about me?"

"Have you discussed them with your doctor?"

"No. This is the first time anything like this has happened."

"Well, call him tomorrow and tell him about them," Andrew ordered. "You probably just need more calcium."

She sighed. "What I need is a better body."

"Nonsense." Andrew's eyes slipped over hers with a hot gleam of interest he made no effort to disguise. "The one you have is great. It just needs to be fine-tuned."

"Not by milk," she objected. "I loathe milk. I'll take some calcium tablets."

"Not before you check with your doctor," Andrew repeated. "The book says that calcium pills only work in the presence of vitamin D, and too much vitamin D can be harmful to the baby."

"Too much knowledge can be harmful to one's peace of mind," Lucy complained. "It seems like everything we eat or breathe is liable to cause something awful to happen."

"Not the food I put in your refrigerator."

"Oh, great. I can have the choice of eating things that taste like grass or mildew or dying of cancer."

"You're just out of sorts because your leg hurts. Or else you're having a mood swing." His very reasonableness irritated her.

"I am not indulging in a mood swing!" she gritted out.

"Of course you aren't," he agreed with a promptness that merely intensified her anger. "It's your hormones doing it. You really have very little control over it."

"Oh?" Lucy's natural sense of humor began to surface at his earnest expression. "Does that mean my emotional reactions are not my fault?"

"Well . . ." He eyed her cautiously.

"Say, for example, I want to have a mood swing the next time you mention that book and I lay violent hands on you."

"You can lay hands on me anytime," he answered promptly, and Lucy gave up. It was much too nice a day to argue. The sun was shining, the air was crisp and invigorating, the fallen leaves crunched underfoot and she was with a man she liked.

"I like you, Andrew Killion." She smiled at him and then jumped smack into the middle of a huge pile of leaves on the sidewalk, missing his arrested expression at her words.

"Excuse me, lady, but I got a shipment here for a Lucy Hartford." The deliveryman shoved a bill of lading at her. "Sign here."

Lucy scrawled her signature, gave him an absent smile and turned back to the knitting pattern she was trying to decipher.

"But where do you want it, lady?" the man demanded impatiently.

"Just put it here." She gestured to the counter in front of her. "I'll take care of it later."

"Not hardly." The man grimaced. "It's way too big."

"Too big?" Lucy gave him her full attention. "What on earth did the company pack the yarn in that it won't fit on my counter?"

"I don't know about no yarn. What I got is a bed and a mattress and the bill of lading says I'm to set it up. So, where do you want it set up?" He glanced around the comfortably crowded shop.

"Let me see that." Lucy reached for the receipt she'd just signed. Sure enough, it listed one bed. She looked at the top of the page. The name Andrew Killion leaped out at her. Andrew had actually bought her a bed. Despite the fact that he was in San Francisco, he'd taken the time to try and come up with a solution to her tiredness. The unexpected feeling of being cherished warmed her.

"Lady?" the deliveryman prodded. "I do have other deliveries to make, you know."

"You can set it up in the storeroom. I'll show you." She led the way through the shop and into the sagging back room.

"Right there, I think." Lucy pointed to the open space under the small window.

"Fine," the man said. "You push those boxes out of the way and me'n Harry'll bring it in."

Lucy shoved boxes of yarn and tapestry wool aside and then perched on the edge of her desk to watch.

While she wasn't sure if it was a good idea to accept gifts from Andrew, she had no intention of turning this one down. It would be an incredible luxury to be able to steal back here at lunchtime and take a quick nap. And with her new clerk due to start on Saturday, she'd be able to.

The two men made short work of assembling the bed.

"The instruction booklet's here." The man handed it to Lucy.

"I certainly don't need that." She chuckled. "I can fall asleep anywhere these days."

"Not for that," the man contradicted. "To tell you how to raise either end."

"You mean it's electric?" Lucy looked closer. Sure enough, there was a cord hanging down.

"Yeah, lady. Like they have in hospitals. Well, if that's all . . ."

"Fine," Lucy muttered, hardly noticing when the men left. She was too enthralled with the bed. Sitting down on it, she bounced tentatively and then found the control on the side and proceeded to raise first the head and then the foot.

"Ah, Disneyland East, as I live and breathe." Annie eyed her indulgently from the doorway. "Not but what it isn't a good idea."

"It certainly is." Lucy leaned back and immediately felt her eyelids start to close. "But it wasn't my good idea. It was Andrew's."

"Speaking of Andrew, where's he been this past week?"

"San Francisco." Lucy quit fighting and let her eyelids close.

"Boy, I've heard of men running when they found out they were going to be fathers, but the whole length of the country?"

"Don't be silly," Lucy told her. "He *wants* to be a father. That's half my problem. And he's in Frisco because of some problems with the construction of a building he designed."

"Wants to be a father?" Annie probed with an avid curiosity.

"But *I* don't want to talk about it," Lucy replied, having no intention of discussing the intricacy of the situation with anyone, even a close friend like Annie.

"He's your hunk," Annie said cheerfully. "Why don't you try out your bed? I'll give you a shriek if I need you."

"Thanks, Annie." Lucy's voice sounded far away to her own ears. It was sheer bliss to be able to give in to the lassitude spreading through her.

It seemed no more than minutes later to Lucy's sleep-drugged mind when Annie gently shook her.

"Lucy, I hate to bother you, but Bob Witton is here."

"Bob?" Lucy forced her sluggish mind into full consciousness. "He isn't supposed to be here until this afternoon."

"He is," Annie explained.

"I know. I just said that." Lucy groggily sat up and shook her head, trying to clear it.

"No, I mean he is here this afternoon. It's past three. You've been asleep for hours."

"I feel like I've been dead." She got to her feet and, staggering over to the small refrigerator along the wall, extracted a soft drink. Opening it, she took a long swallow of the icy liquid and then held the cold can against her forehead. The chill penetrated her skin, helping to further rouse her.

"You okay?" Annie eyed her worriedly.

"Sure. Just a little spaced." She yawned. "It'll wear off in a minute. Tell Bob I'm coming, would you?"

"Take your time," Annie advised. "Considering what that inventory-control package he's selling you costs, he won't mind."

Wasn't that the truth, Lucy thought with a grimace. Computers might be great labor-saving devices, but no one could claim they were cheap. She took another sip of the cola, combed her thick hair off her forehead with her fingers and slipped her feet back into her shoes.

She found Bob powering up the small computer she kept beside the cash register.

"Ah, there you are." He gave her a warm smile that hinted that he wanted to be considered as something more than merely an excellent salesman glad to see a good customer.

Curiously, almost as if she'd never seen him before, Lucy studied him. He was a very attractive man, almost classically handsome with his warm brown eyes and honey-colored hair. His smile was wide, genuine and displayed his straight white teeth to perfection. It was the face of a man most women would find very desirable. So why did he leave her cold? The question nagged at her like a toothache that wouldn't go away. Why did she keep seeing another face superimposed on Bob's? A leaner one with brilliant blue eyes. A chill of fear slithered over her skin, raising goose bumps as it went. What was happening to her? Why did she keep thinking of Andrew when looking at Bob? Was it because of the kisses they'd shared? Or maybe it was because of the life they'd created. But whatever the reason, Lucy knew she had to take steps to combat it. She needed to put Andrew back into perspective, and perhaps Bob could help her do that. She returned his smile with a warm one of her own.

It was all the encouragement he needed. While explaining how her software worked, he also managed to subtly drive home the message that he found her very attractive and would like to get to know her better. There was nothing threatening in his actions, and Lucy forced herself to respond, telling herself that it was for her own good. As a result, when Bob left the store, he left with her promise to have dinner with him after work on Friday.

"Was that wise?" Annie watched the door close after Bob.

"What? Eating out?"

"With another man," Annie corrected. "Does Bob know about Andrew?"

"No, but why should he? All I intend to do is to have a meal with Bob, not get involved emotionally."

"But does Bob know that?" Annie asked shrewdly.

"I hate to disillusion you, but the singles scene isn't as torrid as Hollywood would have us believe—at least, not in Northport. Around here the men don't try to talk you into bed until the third or fourth date."

"That wasn't what I meant, and you know it," Annie said. "I just hope you know what you're doing. Your hunk isn't going to like this."

"First of all, Andrew isn't my anything. Secondly, he doesn't have the right to object, and lastly, he isn't here to object."

She'd been wrong, Lucy thought Friday evening as she sat across from Bob in the restaurant. Andrew might not be there in person, but his memory certainly lingered on. For some reason she seemed totally unable to put him out of her mind—a set of circumstances that not only annoyed her, but made her feel guilty, as well. Bob was a very nice man who deserved to be seen as himself and not as a pallid copy of Andrew's more vivid masculinity.

Lucy tried to force herself to concentrate on what Bob was saying. The problem was that her interest in computers was limited to what they could do for her in the shop. As far as she was concerned, how the computer accomplished what it did was irrelevant. Unfortunately Bob didn't share her opinion. He not only found the inside of a computer fascinating, but he was determined to share that fascination with her in excruciating detail.

Lucy swallowed a sigh, wondering at what point she could end the evening without hurting his feelings—something she had no intention of doing. It wasn't Bob's fault she found him boring. She'd known about his utter absorption in computers before she'd accepted this dinner date. She'd simply forgotten about it in her desire to oust Andrew's image from her mind.

Lucy's eyes widened as Bob took a pack of cigarettes out of his pocket, extracted one and lit it. She'd never objected before when he'd smoked around her, so what could she say now? *Excuse me, but the smell of cigarette smoke makes me want to throw up?* Although it wasn't just the smell of the cigarette smoke that was making her sick, she admitted fairly. If she hadn't indulged in a pizza with everything on it . . . She swallowed uneasily as the first whiff of smoke reached her and her already queasy stomach lurched in protest. Gracefully bringing the date to a close was no longer a consideration. She needed to get home. Now.

"I'm sorry, Bob—" she interrupted his monologue on the latest in microchips "—but I feel a little strange. Would you mind if I cut short our evening?"

"No, of course not." He gave her a warmly understanding smile that made her feel like a heel. He crushed out his cigarette, tossed a tip beside their empty pizza pan and took her arm.

"You're probably just tired."

"Probably," she replied. "The shop was certainly busy today."

"It always is. That place is a regular little gold mine," he said admiringly. "It's amazing how many women fool around with their hands."

"Yup," Lucy agreed blandly, feeling no compulsion to react to his patronizing words—a fact that further confused her. If Andrew had made such an idiotic comment, she'd have been all over him. So, why didn't it bother her when Bob did it?

She worried the question around in her mind on the short drive home, but she was no closer to an answer when they arrived than she'd been when they started.

"Thank you for dinner, Bob." Lucy's polite smile also served to put him at a slight distance. She wasn't quite sure why, but she found the thought of kissing him untenable. "I had a lovely time," she added as he walked her to her front door.

"Me too. We'll have to do it again sometime. How about next Friday?"

"Well—"

"It's about time you got home!" The husky voice came from the deep shadows at the end of the porch. "The store closed hours ago. Where have you been?" Andrew demanded, totally ignoring Bob.

Lucy's instinctive pleasure at the sound of Andrew's voice began to dissolve under the impact of his words. He might be the father of her baby, but that certainly didn't give him any rights where she was concerned—especially, where she was concerned.

"Lucy and I went out to eat." Bob, obviously confused at Andrew's appearance, tried to smooth things over.

"Of all the stupid... You should be home resting, not out carousing until all hours of the night," Andrew snapped.

"Say, who are you?" Bob squinted into the shadows. "Her father?"

Andrew walked under the dim porch light and Bob's eyes widened.

"No, definitely not her father," he muttered, eyeing with misgivings the tailored perfection of Andrew's gray suit and the authority stamped on his features.

"He's . . ." Lucy began weakly.

"I'm the father of the baby she's carrying," Andrew said flatly.

"What!" Bob yelped. He looked at Lucy as if he'd never seen her before. As perhaps he hadn't, Lucy thought in embarrassed resignation.

"Say, listen, I'm sorry, buddy." Bob backed off the porch. "I certainly didn't mean to cause any trouble. Why, I didn't even know Lucy was serious about anybody."

"I am not serious about him," Lucy retorted, tired of being ignored.

"Then you should be," Bob chided her. "I mean, babies are heavy business, and you shouldn't be creating them lightly."

"Lightly!" Lucy squawked as Bob, with one last apologetic look at Andrew, left.

"The man's right, you know," Andrew stated.

"Right?" Lucy glared at him. "He doesn't have one single aspect of this whole damn situation right. Why, do you know what he thinks? That you and I are lovers." The very excitement the idea brought in its wake intensified her anger. "You are the most aggravating man—and not only that, but you're ruining my social life!" she yelled.

"If you wanted to eat out, why didn't you say so? I would have taken you out."

"You don't eat out. You graze out on those vile health-food concoctions. You—" She gasped as her stomach suddenly revolted.

Desperately running to the side of the porch, she leaned over into the shrubbery and lost her dinner.

"I'm never going to survive this pregnancy," she moaned, staggering over to the porch swing and sinking down on it.

"Actually, you should be glad you're so nauseated," Andrew said, "because the book says that's a sign that the baby is developing normally."

"Why, you..." Lucy sputtered, inarticulate with rage. That he would dare to mention that damned book at a time like this! She flung her purse at him. Andrew ducked and it sailed over his head and into the shrubs.

Seven

Lucy stared at Andrew's wary face in shocked surprise. What on earth was the matter with her? She never lost her temper. And yet, for a moment there, all she'd wanted was to smack him—hard. The fact that he was being aggravating was no excuse. She dealt with far more aggravating people in the shop all the time, and she managed to control the urge to throttle them.

"I'm sorry," she muttered, "but when you mentioned that blasted book on top of everything else..."

"What 'everything else'?" Andrew scoffed. "You're the one who was out living it up while I was sitting here in the dark worrying about you."

"There's a porch light," she pointed out, as she considered his words. She hadn't had anyone worrying about what time she got home since she'd moved into her own apartment almost fifteen years ago; and she wasn't sure that she

wanted Andrew worrying now. It was simply one more ten-
dril tying them together.

"It might as well be dark," Andrew grumbled with a dis-
paraging look at the fifteen-watt bulb beside the door. "I'll
replace it in the morning with something more powerful."

"No, you won't. I like its soft glow, and since the only
time I ever use my front door is when someone is with me,
it doesn't matter if it doesn't give off much light. And I
wasn't out living it up," she ended on a wail. "I was out
being bored out of my mind. I now know more about computers than I ever wanted to know. And when I finally
managed to end the blasted date, I get home to find you
lurking on my front porch." She sniffed disconsolately as a
sense of ill-usage filled her.

"My poor angel." Andrew reached out and pulled her
unresisting body into his arms. "So you're the victim in all
this?" A thread of laughter colored his voice.

"Don't mock me." Lucy snuggled closer. It felt so good
to be in his arms. So right. As if this were where she'd really
wanted to be all evening instead of pretending that she was
enjoying another man's company.

"I'd better get inside." She tried to sound decisive and
failed dismally. "I want to get to bed before my stomach
decides to stage an encore."

"Good idea." Andrew gently brushed a kiss across her
forehead. His breath warmed her skin a second before his
lips touched it, and Lucy felt a jolt of desire shake her at his
casual salute. She held herself immobile for a long second
out of time as she savored the exquisite sensation.

"If you'll give me your key..." Andrew prodded.

"Key? Oh. Yes, the key." She frowned. "Well, you see,
it's in my purse and..."

"And you threw it at me," he finished. He leaned over
the railing and squinted into the thick shrubs. "You definitely need a stronger wattage," he muttered. "I can't...

Aha!'' His voice rose in triumph as he fished an object out of the bushes. ''Your purse, madame.''

Lucy took it, frowning when she realized that it was empty. The clasp had come open when she'd flung it and the contents had spilled out. She peered around Andrew at the very dark bushes.

''Now what's the matter?'' Andrew asked indulgently.

Lucy turned her purse upside down to illustrate just what was the matter.

''Oh.'' Andrew turned and followed her gaze to the shrubbery. ''This could be a problem. Not only is it dark as Hades by the ground, but you lost your dinner over that railing and I for one have no desire to go crawling around down there.''

''Nobody's asking you to. Just give me the spare key you used to let yourself in all those other times.''

''If you'll remember correctly, you demanded I give it back. I left it on your bedside table.''

''Great.'' Lucy sighed. ''That must be the only time you've ever listened to me.''

''Well, at least that makes me one up on you. You've never listened to me even once,'' he shot back.

''I could break a window.'' Lucy suggested, ignoring his crack.

''Bad idea. Not only would you have to sleep in a house with an open window, but you'd have to stay home until you could get a glazier out here to replace it. And finding someone willing to come out on a Saturday morning might not be easy.''

''And tomorrow's our busiest day.'' Lucy eyed Andrew speculatively. ''You wouldn't be willing to house-sit, would you? Just until—''

''Sorry, I can't. I have an appointment tomorrow morning at eight about a new high-rise I'm designing.''

''On Saturday?''

"He's Japanese," Andrew said, as if that explained everything. "But didn't you tell me once that you had a spare key?"

"Sure, in the shop," Lucy replied promptly. "Unfortunately, the key to said shop now resides somewhere in the bushes."

"Does Annie have a key to the shop?"

"Uh-huh." She nodded. "But she always plays bingo on Friday and Saturday nights, and I haven't the vaguest idea where she plays. It could be midnight before she gets home. I guess it'll have to be a hotel. I can come back in the morning once it's light and find the keys easily enough."

"You can't go to a motel without luggage."

"Of course I can." She ignored her own doubts. "I'll simply explain what happened."

"How are you going to get there?"

"You'll take me?" she suggested.

"Wrong. I have no intention of encouraging idiocy."

"Then I'll take a cab," she stated firmly.

"How are you going to pay for it?" Andrew's smug expression made her long to fling her purse at him again.

"I know how to get housing for the night," she snapped. "I'll murder you and the police'll arrest me and I can sleep at the jail."

"You'd never be able to post bail in time to open the shop tomorrow."

Lucy sighed. "I knew there had to be a catch to such a lovely idea. Then I guess I'm going to spend the night on my porch swing."

"Wrong again." Andrew took her arm and hustled her down the steps. "You're going to spend the evening in my guest room. Where," he added on an aggrieved note, "if you'd been the least bit reasonable, you'd already be living."

"I'm not sure...." Lucy balked at climbing into his car even though she was intensely curious to see where he lived. The very force of that intensity made her hesitant.

"I am." He bundled her into the car.

And that's that, Lucy thought in wry amusement.

"Buckle your seat belt." Andrew turned the key in the ignition and the Porsche throbbed to life.

Lucy studied the dials on the dashboard enviously. She'd wanted to buy a Corvette when she'd traded her old car in last year, but had finally decided that the Voyager with its pop-out seats was a much more sensible purchase for someone in her circumstances.

"You like sports cars?" Andrew caught her expression.

"Who doesn't? But you know this is not the kind of car one puts a baby in."

"Hmm?" Andrew checked the traffic and turned onto Jericho Turnpike.

"Not only is there no room for the tons of equipment they need, but babies have a nasty habit of throwing up—and these seats are real leather." She ran her hand reverently over the back of hers.

"So do you, and you're here."

Lucy winced. "That was a low blow."

"My poor angel." Andrew laughed. "Now close your eyes and go to sleep."

She obediently closed her eyes, and almost immediately drifted into a drowsy state of semiconscious contentment—a state that lasted until Andrew pulled the car into a parking space and cut the engine.

"Come on, Lucy." He lightly brushed his knuckles across her cheek. "We're here."

Lucy opened her eyes and peered around blearily. They appeared to be in a well-lit underground parking garage.

"Where's here?" she asked around an enormous yawn.

"My apartment building." He unsnapped her seat belt, then leaned across her and pushed open the car door. His arm brushed against her breasts, sending a shock of sensation through her that jerked her to instant awareness. Hastily she climbed out of the car, eager to escape the subtle torture of his touch.

"Where exactly are we?" she questioned.

"Manhattan." He followed her into the elevator and pushed a button.

Lucy's eyes widened as the elevator shot upward, leaving her stomach behind. None too soon it came to a halt, and she winced as she noticed what floor they were on.

"What's the matter?" asked Andrew.

"Ever since I saw that movie about the fire in the skyscraper, I get nervous above the second floor. Can you imagine trying to run down twenty-five flights of stairs if there were a fire?"

"Easier than I can imagine trying to run *up* twenty-five flights of stairs." He unlocked the door of an apartment about fifty feet away from the elevator.

Curious, Lucy stepped inside and peered around the spacious entrance hall. She wasn't sure what she'd been expecting, but this wasn't it.

"You don't like it?"

"It's not that. It . . . just isn't you," she finally said, gesturing toward the living room full of chrome, leather and glass.

"Oh?" Andrew eyed her thoughtfully. "And what is me?"

"Well . . ." She studied him a moment. "I suppose I expected Queen Anne or Regency furniture. Solid, enduring . . . Oh, I don't know." She was suddenly uneasy at his intense stare. "I suppose I'm being fanciful."

"Actually, you're rather perceptive. My ex-wife decorated the apartment. It reflects her tastes, not mine. I'll show you your bedroom."

Lucy frowned as she followed him down the hallway. His ex-wife had decorated the apartment, and he hadn't changed anything despite the fact that it didn't reflect his tastes. Why? Because he missed her? Or because he was busy with other things and simply didn't care enough to redecorate? Lucy sighed, wishing there were some way of knowing just how important his ex-wife was to him. If there were any possibility of the woman reappearing in his life it could affect the baby, she reasoned, mentally justifying her intense curiosity.

"Here you are." Andrew pushed open a door and, reaching inside, flipped on the light.

"Good Lord!" Lucy blinked at the sight of the psychedelic posters on the opposite wall. "There appear to be hidden depths to your ex-wife's psyche. Depths better left unexplored."

"Don't be ridiculous. Amanda didn't do this. She did."

"She?" Lucy asked. Had Andrew had a live-in lover at sometime in the not-too-distant past? But if he'd had a live-in lover, surely she'd have shared his bed?

"Miss Day. Since she'd agreed to live here for nine months, I told her she could have the room redecorated any way she wanted and this was what she wanted."

"Purple walls, black carpeting and a silver ceiling?" Lucy stared at the ceiling in fascination. "Personally, if I'd been you, the minute I saw this mess, I'd have canceled the contract. There's obviously a strong streak of instability in Miss Day's makeup."

"She was going to start work on her Ph.D. in music history," he explained to excuse her. "And she had perfect pitch."

Lucy bit back a nasty crack. She refused to keep apologizing just because she couldn't carry a tune.

"Ah, well." He sighed. "It's a moot point at this juncture. Why don't you climb into bed, and I'll make you a nice cup of weak chamomile tea?"

"Did your ex-wife leave any clothes behind?" Lucy asked.

"If she had, after five years she's had plenty of time to retrieve them. Why?"

Lucy felt a surge of relief at his words. After five years he should be over the pain of his divorce. "Because I just realized that I don't have a nightgown," she said.

"Hmm." His eyes began to gleam, and she felt a shiver of excitement at the desire she saw in them. "How about one of my pajama tops?" he suggested.

"Sounds good."

"I'll get that and your tea."

"Would you give me the pajamas first and hold the tea for about ten minutes?" she asked, wanting to be safely in bed before he came back.

She was, barely. She'd just slipped between the black satin sheets and had pulled the covers up, trying to disguise the fact that the first button of his oversize pajama top was below her breasts, when he returned.

All it took was one quick look at Andrew's face as he handed her the cup of tea to convince her that she'd been unsuccessful. His eyes glittered with hunger, and his features had hardened into sharply delineated planes.

Lucy stared down into the misty tendrils of steam rising from her cup feeling confused, uncertain and excited. Absently she took a sip of her tea and then gasped as the scalding liquid burned her mouth.

"It's hot," she choked out, dropping the sheet.

"Of course it's hot." Andrew rescued the cup from her shaking hand, setting it on the Lucite cube that functioned as a bedside table and sat down beside her.

"Poor angel." Andrew cupped her chin and studied her flushed face. "This just isn't your day, is it?"

"Forget today," she grumbled. "This isn't my life."

"Nonsense. It's a great life."

"Now *that* has a ring to it," she said ruefully.

Andrew tipped her head back and ordered, "Stick out your tongue."

Lucy laughed. "Is this going to get kinky?"

"Stick it out," he repeated. "I want to see if you've damaged it."

"I've probably burned off all my taste buds—which might be an advantage around this place. At least I won't have to actually taste all that mildew-flavored grass you serve."

"Lucy!"

"Oh, for heaven's sake!" She stuck out her tongue. A curious feeling twisted in her chest at the absorbed expression on Andrew's face as he studied it. He looked so endearingly earnest.

"It looks all right," he announced slowly.

"Thank you, Dr. Killion."

"Now, scoot down under the covers and I'll tuck you in."

Lucy obediently scooted.

Andrew's fingers brushed against her rib cage as he started to pull the sheets up. He paused as he reached her breasts and his eyes lingered on the wide V of skin exposed by his pajama top.

Mesmerized, Lucy watched his lips curl in a sensual twist. She shifted slightly and her leg pressed up against his, trapping her. But it wasn't a threatening sensation. Far from it. She felt secure, protected and desired. Especially desired. There was no mistaking the expression on his face. He was seeing her, Lucy Hartford—not some nameless female who happened to be carrying his baby. The intoxicating thought bubbled through her like the effervescence of vintage champagne.

"You have such exquisite skin." Andrew slowly traced along her collarbone with a fingertip, and Lucy jumped as the friction sent a shower of sparks through her. His finger dipped lower, along the bodice opening. It paused at the beginning of the swell of her breast, and Lucy held her breath in anticipation.

"You feel like rose petals that have been basking in the sun—warm and velvety." He lowered his head and pressed his lips against the soft skin next to his finger.

Heat curled through Lucy and she stared down at his bent head, her eyes caught by the inky blackness of his hair. Fascinated, she reached out and touched it. It felt silky and she threaded her finger through it.

As if encouraged by her action, Andrew slipped the top pajama button open and pushed the material aside, exposing her breasts to his avid gaze.

Lucy felt the warmth of his breath across her skin and her nipples tightened longingly.

Slowly, tentatively, as if afraid to hurt her, he brushed his thumb over the tight peaks, and she gasped in pleasure. Her pregnancy seemed to have made her breasts much more sensitive than they normally were.

"Andrew?" Her thin voice was part plea and part demand and he responded by cupping her breast in his hand and capturing the swollen tip in his mouth. As the warm dampness of his tongue slid over it, Lucy pushed her fingers into his hair and grasped his head, holding him close. Andrew rewarded her small act of aggressiveness by suckling on the throbbing breast.

Lucy twisted beneath the impact of the sensation tearing through her, and the remaining buttons on her pajama top slipped free.

He pulled the sheet down farther and slowly, ever so slowly, pushed aside the gaping top. Placing his warm, callused palm over her abdomen with an almost reverent expression on his face, he lowered his head and began to paint designs on her belly with the tip of his tongue.

"Andrew, please," she gasped. "I want—" Her voice echoed harshly in her ears, shocking her to sudden awareness. The chill of reality poured over her, dousing her excitement and catapulting her back to reality.

What was the matter with her? she wondered, condemning herself. She was reacting to Andrew with a mindless intensity that bordered on obsession. She'd never felt anything like this in her life. It was as if the safe stream she'd always enjoyed wading in had suddenly been swallowed up in flood waters and she'd been swept away by a raging current.

"No." She weakly repudiated both the feeling and the implication of that feeling. It was just because she was pregnant and her emotions were already churned up, she assured herself. That was what had added the extra dimension to Andrew's lovemaking.

The rigidity of her body finally penetrated his total absorption. He raised his head and stared down at her, a curiously blank expression on his face.

As she watched, the blankness faded. "Did I hurt you?" His voice was slightly hoarse.

"Oh, no," she answered honestly. "You were...I was..."

"Never mind." He smiled tenderly at her. "I get the idea. I felt the same way. I take it your poor tummy is acting up again?"

Lucy smiled weakly, ashamed of herself for taking the easy way out, but too confused to come up with a plausible lie, especially considering the fact that she wasn't sure exactly what the problem was.

Andrew slowly pulled the covers up under her chin.

"Sleep tight. Don't let the bedbugs bite."

"Bedbugs?" She eyed him in fascination. "Do you have bedbugs?"

"I've never even seen one. That used to be what one of my foster mothers would say when we kids went to bed. Actually—" his face hardened for a fraction of a second "—looking back on it, she might really have had bedbugs."

"Foster mother?" Lucy latched on to the words. "What were you doing with foster parents?"

"Living. Or more precisely, surviving."

"You're an orphan?" Lucy asked, trying to reconcile what she knew of Andrew Killion with this unexpected revelation.

"No. Most kids in foster care aren't. I had a mother whose second husband didn't want another man's kid around the house so she dumped me in foster care."

"And your father?" Lucy asked, trying to read his expression.

"Didn't come home from Korea." He shrugged. "A common enough tale and long finished. Now go to sleep. You need your rest."

Lucy watched him leave, her mind a seething mass of conjecture. She felt confused and disoriented. Not only did she have the problem of her inexplicable reaction to Andrew's lovemaking to deal with, but there was also the startling self-revelation that he'd so casually dropped into the conversation.

Thoughtfully she stared at the chrome light fixture overhead, which gleamed softly as it reflected the full moon. Andrew might say that his having been raised in foster care was history, but it wasn't. Not really. The aftereffects lingered on, helping to explain why he was so emphatic about having custody of his own child and why, too, he could believe that a surrogate would fall in with his plans and give up her child. After all, his own mother had abandoned him.

Lucy's heart ached for the hurt little boy Andrew must have been. He deserved better. Then and now. He deserved a real family, but the only way she could accomplish that was to give him her baby. She sighed. What a tangled mess. But even as complicated as the situation was, Lucy no longer regretted the fact that Andrew was the father of her baby. He was the most vividly masculine man she'd ever met; and while that was by no means all good, certain aspects of it certainly were. She stretched luxuriously, remembering his kiss, and it was with the memory of it lingering in her mind that she slipped into a deep, dreamless sleep.

She awoke the next morning to find a note from Andrew on the bedside table saying that he'd had to leave for his early meeting and to make sure she ate before she left. Stapled to the note was a hundred-dollar bill she was to use to pay a taxi to take her home.

Lucy worriedly studied his bold, black scrawl. Why hadn't he woken her before he'd left? Could it be that he regretted what had almost happened last night and was using his absence to make the point?

"And the situation could be exactly what he said it was," she lectured the disgusting-looking bowl of nuts and twigs she'd found sitting on the kitchen table. It was obvious that he worked too hard. He needed to slow down and live a little.

A flush stained her cheeks as her mind obligingly recalled just how much they'd almost lived last night. Determinedly, she banished the memory and reached for the cereal. She didn't have time to wallow in might-have-beens. She had to get to the store.

She made it there in good time, but only by dint of encouraging the homicidal tendencies of the cabbie who drove her out to Long Island. To her relief, her stomach made no objections to the hair-raising ride, and she was beginning to think that her nausea really was a thing of the past—as long as she remembered to avoid cigarette smoke and anchovies, that was.

The day turned out to be even more hectic than Saturdays usually were. Not only was the store swamped with customers, but the new salesclerk she'd hired seemed to require more help than she gave. But Lucy maintained a calm front through it all, knowing that the situation would quickly improve.

"I'm back." Annie stashed her purse under the counter. "Why don't you go get something to eat. It's after one."

Lucy looked up from the skeins of violet yarn she was counting and gave Annie an absent smile. "Not right now. I want to get some of the stock replaced while things aren't so busy. We've—"

She turned as the door chimes tinkled and a surge of pleasure went through her at the sight of Andrew silhouetted in the doorway.

"Ah-hah! So that's what you were waiting for," Annie whispered. "The hunk."

"Don't call him that. He might hear," Lucy whispered back, watching Andrew as he crossed the shop toward her. He looked calm and vaguely pleased with himself.

"Good afternoon, Annie." Andrew gave the older woman a gleaming smile. "Has Lucy eaten yet?"

"No, Lucy hasn't," Lucy answered for herself. "And if you're about to tell me that you've brought lunch—" she nodded toward the sacks in his hands "—then she probably won't. I am definitely not in the mood for more mildew."

"Mildew?" Annie frowned in confusion. "You mean like penicillin grows on bread mold?"

Lucy chuckled. "Something like that."

"Ha! Just for that, I'm tempted not to let you have the dessert I brought you," Andrew shot back.

"Let me guess. Carob brownies with wheat nuts and Tofu icing?"

He reached into one of the bags and pulled out a small container with a gesture reminiscent of a magician pulling a rabbit out of a hat.

"I brought you a pint of almond-fudge ice cream," he said.

"Wrong. You brought me gastronomical ambrosia." Lucy grabbed for it, missed when he raised it over his head, and landed against his hard chest. The warm, musky scent of his skin flooded her nostrils.

"First the main course, then dessert." Andrew held on to the ice cream.

"Very wise," an elderly lady perusing the tapestry canvases near the counter remarked. "So many of you young things have no idea of proper nutrition." She gave Lucy a reproving look over the top of her reading glasses.

Lucy smiled back, unfazed. She'd put up with all kinds of disapproval to get her hands on a whole pint of almond fudge.

"Come on, Andrew. Let's eat." She started toward the back room.

"Hey, where'd Lydia go?" Annie called after her.

"She's memorizing stock in the room full of cotton yarns. Call me if you need me."

"Who's Lydia?" Andrew asked as he handed her her lunch—a pita sandwich filled with something she felt it would be better not to inquire too closely about.

Lucy took a bite, frowning as the taste registered. She swallowed and then took a long drink of the opened can of orange juice sitting on her desk.

"You should be drinking milk," he objected.

"This is calcium-fortified orange juice, and Lydia is my new clerk. She's a find."

"In what way?"

"She's extremely knowledgeable about all kinds of needlework, and since she doesn't need money, she only wants to work part-time."

"If she doesn't need the money, why is she working at all? Boredom?"

"More lack of purpose. You see, her husband of twenty-eight years died suddenly of a massive heart attack at Easter, and while she's worked through the worst of the grief, she's lonely. Her oldest child lives in California and her youngest is in college in Boston. Working here gives her a place to go where she feels needed, and she enjoys the work. It's a great deal for both of us."

"Sounds like it," Andrew approved.

"And when you add to that a pint of almond fudge..." Lucy eyed the container beside him covetously.

"First eat your—"

"No, don't tell me what it is. I really don't want to know. In this case I have the feeling that ignorance really is bliss."

"If that's true, you have to be the most blissfully inclined person about food that I've ever met," Andrew said wryly.

"Quit insulting my sense of survival and tell me how your meeting went."

"Quite well, and mercifully brief, since he has a flight back to Tokyo later this afternoon. I'm free for the rest of the day so I brought my sketch pad. I thought I'd rough out some ideas for your addition while you take a nap."

"One does not nap around here on a Saturday."

''Then you can lie down for a few minutes and let the tension drain away.''

But Lucy found that when she did lie down more than her tension slipped away. Her consciousness did, too, and she fell into a heavy sleep.

Eight

Over an hour later, Lucy slowly surfaced through layers of satisfying sleep. She lay for a few minutes with her eyes still closed, savoring the feeling of well-being that blanketed her. Cautiously she shifted slightly, but nothing disturbed her peace. Her stomach remained calm, and there wasn't so much as a twitch of a cramp in her legs.

It was the muted sounds of the customers in the shop filtering through the closed door which finally prodded her into action. She knew she had no business sleeping on a Saturday. Poor Annie must be rushed off her feet.

Lucy sat up and swung her legs over the side of the bed. She ran her fingers through her tousled hair, brushing the rich brown strands off her pale forehead. Yawning prodigiously, she stood up and pulled her cream Aryan knit pullover down over the unbuttoned waistband of her brown slacks.

Suddenly remembering Andrew, she glanced around the crowded storeroom, but the only evidence that he'd ever been there was the pad of drawing paper lying on her desk.

Curious, she walked over and looked down at it, whistling soundlessly as she saw what he'd drawn. Andrew Killion was a very talented artist if this picture was anything to go by. She reached out and tentatively touched the small figure in the playpen he'd put in the middle of a large, multiwindowed nursery.

Lucy looked around her decrepit storeroom, trying to visualize what he'd drawn to take its place. Her imagination wasn't equal to the task.

Her eyes returned to the tiny baby in the playpen, and she wondered how Andrew visualized their child. It was impossible to tell from the picture. Perhaps their baby would have Andrew's artistic abilities. She smiled as in her mind an image of a man with her hair and Andrew's build formed. He was wearing a paint-stained smock and daubing at an oversize canvas. Lucy blinked as the figure turned his head, and she saw that he was missing his right ear.

"Better he should be a doctor," she muttered, and better she should get out into the shop where she was undoubtedly needed.

She slipped her feet into her flats, splashed water on her face from the chipped sink in the corner and then hurried out.

To her relief, everything seemed to be under control. Her new clerk was checking someone out at the cash register and Annie was explaining something to an elderly woman holding an armful of pale blue knitting yarn.

With an encouraging smile at Lydia, Lucy walked through the room full of tapestry yarns toward the front of the store. A quick surge of pleasure filled her as she caught sight of Andrew standing in a corner talking to a customer.

Hungrily she studied him, soaking up the vibrancy of his personality like a sponge. His black hair was faintly tousled and the cleanly chiseled planes of his face were outlined against the rainbow assortment of mohair yarns lining the wall behind him.

Her eyes dropped to his neck to linger on the deep V of tanned skin revealed by his partially unbuttoned white shirt. At some point he'd discarded his tie and suit jacket and had rolled up his shirt sleeves. A strand of the deep red yarn he was holding was curled around his long fingers.

Lucy let her breath out in a long, shuddering sigh as she remembered the feel of those fingers cupping her breasts. A tingling awareness shot through her at the evocative memory. Doing her best to ignore it, Lucy walked over to the pair.

"Feeling better?" Andrew gave her a searching look, the intimacy of it momentarily shutting out the customer.

"Yes, thanks." She turned to the woman, wondering what she and Andrew had been discussing so intently. "May I help you?" Lucy asked.

"Well..." The woman gave her an uncertain smile. "With my red hair I usually stick to browns or greens when I knit for myself. But this time I decided to be a little more adventurous, and I was trying that color—" she nodded to the yarn Andrew was holding "—up against my face so I could see if it was too awful, when he told me it was."

"That shade of red does nothing for her," Andrew insisted. "It has purple undertones, which make her skin look sallow. If she wants to wear red, and I think it's a good idea—" he smiled reassuringly at the woman "—she should stick to reds with an orange base. Such as this one." He reached behind him, took a skein of yarn off the shelf and held it beside the woman's face. "See what I mean?" he asked.

"He's right," Lucy said slowly. "That shade of red does look quite good on you. It enhances your red hair instead of clashing with it."

"You really think so?" the woman asked wistfully. "I'm so sick of earth tones."

"I really think so," Lucy repeated honestly. "Tell you what. If you get the red yarn and find out once you've got it knitted up that you don't like it, bring it back and I'll give you a new batch of yarn in an earth tone."

"I'll do it," the woman decided. "And I won't be bringing it back. It's about time I started living a little. Thank you for your help." She smiled at Andrew.

"You're welcome." Andrew smiled back and Lucy felt a totally unexpected flash of jealousy shoot through her. She didn't want Andrew smiling at strange women. Or at familiar ones, either, come to that. She only wanted Andrew to smile at her. Her primitive reaction appalled her.

Leaving the woman checking dye-lot numbers on the red yarn, Lucy, closely followed by Andrew, headed toward the back of the store.

"Why were you waiting on that woman?" Lucy probed, once they were safely in the storeroom and away from the curious eyes of her customers.

"I wasn't. At least not precisely." He picked up his notepad and began to write in the margin.

Lucy took a soft drink out of the refrigerator, opened it and took a long, satisfying swallow. "Would you like something to drink?" She peered over his shoulder at his notes. They made no sense to her.

He reached for the can, took a drink and handed it back to her. "Thanks," he muttered absently, continuing to scribble.

Lucy took a second sip, allowing her lips to linger where his had rested as her mind obligingly replayed the feel of his firm lips pressing into hers. She blinked to break the spell and focused instead on her question. "What were you doing in the shop?" she repeated.

"I wanted to check the window in the back room that faces the alley. It occurred to me that if you make this a nursery, then you're going to have a lot of stock with no place to put it. So I thought we could run the addition across the whole rear of the shop. That way half could be for the baby and half for storage."

"Sounds good to me." Lucy nodded approvingly. "I hadn't quite decided what I was going to do about the spare stock. By the way, I really like your drawing of the nursery." She gave praise where it was due.

"Speaking of the baby, what do you think of Arabella?"

Lucy frowned, trying to place the name and failing. "Who's Arabella, and what does she have to do with the baby?"

"No, I meant as a name for our daughter, if she really is a girl."

Our daughter. Lucy savored the sound of the words. They sounded so right, somehow—even if the name didn't.

"If it's a girl, I get to name her Mary Frances, after my grandmothers."

"Both your grandmothers were named Mary Frances?"

"No. One was named Mary and the other Frances, and I like the combination. It has a nice ring to it."

"It does?" he asked dubiously.

"Sure. For example, Aunt Mary Frances or Doctor Mary Frances Hartford or—"

"Doctor Mary Frances Killion," Andrew corrected. "If you get the first name, I get the last. Besides, in this culture, it's still the norm for a child to use her father's name."

"But it'll create all kinds of complications if she and I have different last names," Lucy objected.

"No, it won't. What with the divorce and remarriage rates in this country, I swear that half the kids I know have different last names from their mothers."

"I don't care about them. I care about me. How about if we were to use a hyphen?"

Andrew frowned uncomprehendingly. "A hyphen?"

"Yeah, you know. Call her Mary Frances Hartford-Killion."

"And hope she'd learned to spell it all by the third grade?" Andrew scoffed. "Besides, think of our grandchildren."

"Grandchildren?" Lucy eyed him uncertainly.

"Suppose Mary Frances marries a man who also had a hyphenated name—say, Vanlandingham-Tomlicheck—and neither of them are willing to compromise. We could wind up with grandchildren named Hartford-Killion-Vanlandingham-Tomlicheck."

"I don't think you have to worry," Lucy said dryly. "You're much more likely to wind up in a mental ward first."

"I'm right, and you know it," Andrew insisted. "My child should have my name."

"That's a simplistic viewpoint, although I will admit, you might have a point. Especially if it's a boy."

"Boy or girl, it's still my child and still entitled to my name."

"All right." Lucy threw up her hands in defeat. "We'll use your last name and call her Mary Frances if she's a girl."

"What if it's a boy?"

"Then we won't call him Mary Frances." Lucy grinned at him.

"Since you get to name a girl, I should get to name the baby if it's a boy."

"What did you have in mind?" she asked cautiously, wondering what a man who liked Arabella would choose for a boy.

"Something that doesn't lend itself to ridiculous nicknames. Like...say, John?"

"I like John, but frankly, I'd be a little worried about bathroom jokes. What's your middle name?"

"James."

"James," she repeated thoughtfully. "We could call him Jamie when he's little. What was your father's name?"

"Arthur."

"Arthur." Lucy tested the sound of it. "James Arthur Killion. I like it."

"My father died in Korea," Andrew objected.

"So? I'm sure he didn't do it simply to annoy you," she remarked dryly.

"No, of course not. It's just that I don't remember him at all." Andrew ran his fingers through his hair in frustration.

"Didn't he have any family?" Lucy asked, intensely curious about Andrew's background.

"A father who from all accounts was a recluse. He didn't care for children, although he was a firm believer in shouldering his responsibilities."

"That was his loss," Lucy said, angered by the look of sadness that momentarily shadowed his face.

"No, it was mine," Andrew slowly explained. "You see, my grandfather set up a trust fund which paid a set amount to my mother every month for my expenses."

Lucy frowned. "But I thought you said you were raised in foster care."

"I was. My mother never told Social Services that I had a trust fund. She simply pocketed the check every month. That was why she would never allow me to be adopted. If she had, she'd have lost the money."

"Why of all the selfish . . ." Lucy sputtered indignantly. "She should have been shot."

Andrew chuckled. "Something worse happened. When I graduated from high school, what was left of the trust was to be given to me to help pay for college. She tried to pass my oldest half brother off as me, but since he was barely fifteen at the time, the lawyer for the bank that administered the trust became suspicious and investigated."

"And?" Lucy demanded when he paused.

"It all came out, and I was given the eleven thousand left in the trust."

"And that was it?" Lucy asked in disappointment.

"No, my bloodthirsty little wench. That wasn't it. The bank's lawyers sent a copy of their report to Social Services, who then filed a lawsuit against my mother for all the money they had spent on me since she dumped me on them at the age of two."

"I hope they collected every last penny," Lucy replied angrily, her mind filled with the thought of what Andrew must have gone through as a small child.

"Don't look so fierce." Andrew cupped her chin and dropped a warm kiss on her slightly parted lips. "I survived."

"Children shouldn't survive their childhood. They should enjoy it."

"My child will," Andrew said with a deep satisfaction that warmed her. "You'd never abandon your responsibilities. And your career shouldn't interfere that much. You'll be able to have your child right here at work with you. And speaking of being with you, I wanted to ask you if you're free next Saturday evening."

"Why?"

"I'm going to a charity dinner, and I need to bring a partner. It'll be a chance for you to meet some of my friends."

"I see." Lucy squelched her first burst of excitement and forced herself to consider the situation logically. While she was surprised and very gratified that he was not only willing but seemingly eager to introduce her to his friends and colleagues, a niggling sense of unease about the future filled her. She was becoming much too involved with Andrew. He was slowly infiltrating her work and personal life, and now he seemed intent on involving her in his. But was that really such a good idea? What about later when the baby was born and his focus shifted from the woman who'd carried his child to the child itself? Where would she be then if she allowed herself to become too emotionally involved with him now?

And you might get hit by a car tomorrow and the whole question would be moot, she mocked herself. Everything in life was a risk, and human relationships were no exception. Andrew was worth a few risks, she decided.

"Surely it isn't that big a decision?" he asked, and Lucy caught what she very much feared was a flash of hurt in his eyes—a hurt she hurried to soothe.

"I'd love to come. I was just trying to think what I could wear. My waistline went the way of the great auk."

"That's natural. The book says that thin women show before pudgy ones," Andrew responded comfortingly. "Now, tell me how you want your storeroom designed." He reached out and pulled her down onto the box beside him.

Lucy shivered slightly at the feel of his hard thigh pressing into hers, but she made no move to put distance between them. She liked the physical contact. It made her feel complete somehow.

Forcing herself to focus on his question, she said, "I want shelves. Lots and lots of shelves. I'm tired of having to sift through piles of boxes every time I need something."

"Hmm." Andrew stared off into the distance for a second and then suggested, "We could have a cathedral ceiling with skylights and put a loft around all four walls. That would give you two levels for storage.''

He began to sketch and Lucy happily leaned closer, fascinated by the picture growing under his quickly moving pencil.

Lucy opened her front door almost before the sound of the chimes had faded. It seemed as if she'd been waiting hours for Andrew to arrive, and now that he was here she couldn't wait another second to see him.

Her eyes widened at the imposing sight he made in his dinner jacket. He looked exactly like what he was—a sophisticated, wealthy professional—and she felt vaguely intimidated by the image he was projecting.

"Good evening." She gestured toward her living room. "Would you like a drink?"

"We don't have time. The traffic's heavy on the inbound expressway," he answered absently, his attention focused on her. "I like that dress, especially the collar." He reached out and lightly touched the intricately crocheted cream silk collar. "It makes you look like a cross between a Madonna and a little girl dressed up for her dancing lesson."

"Thank you...I think." Her voice was husky as the brush of his fingers against her neck sent a shower of sparks over her skin.

"Oh, it was most definitely a compliment." The glow in his eyes intensified. "You look perfect. Absolutely perfect."

Lucy gulped, suddenly uneasy at both the desire she saw in his eyes and her own body's reaction to that desire. "It's the dress." She gestured toward the bronze silk. "I just love silk. It makes me feel so..." She broke off as she realized she'd almost said sensuous and then rushed on. "I had the devil of a time finding it. My own clothes are all too tight, and regular maternity clothes are still too big and..."

Andrew leaned forward and effectively stopped the flow of nervous words by the simple expedient of placing his lips over hers.

Surprise held Lucy motionless a fraction of a second and then pleasure poured through her, banishing her uncertainties and making her sway toward him. His arms closed around her and he pulled her closer, cradling her against him.

Lucy's eyes slid shut, the better to savor the sensation of his mouth pressed upon hers. This was the Andrew she knew, she thought in relief. He hadn't changed anything but his clothes.

She shuddered as he ran the tip of his tongue over her bottom lip, and her mouth parted eagerly. Quickly, Andrew's tongue surged inside and began a sensuous stroking movement that made her moan with barely contained delight. Much too soon for her clamoring emotions, he lifted his head and smiled down into her unfocused eyes.

"I missed you this past week," he murmured. "It seems like I haven't had a minute to call my own. But at least I've cleared up the problem in San Francisco."

"I missed you, too," she admitted, forcing herself to step out of the protective circle of his arms.

"And your morning sickness?" he persisted.

"Virtually gone, just like the book said." She picked up a brown silk shawl heavily embroidered with gold thread and draped it across her shoulders, pausing when she noticed his frown.

"It really is gone," she assured him.

"That flimsy scarf isn't any good." He gestured disdainfully at it. "It's October out there. You need a coat."

"It's been such a mild fall that I haven't gotten around to picking up my winter coat from the dry cleaners where it's stored."

"Wear that jacket I saw hanging in the front closet."

"Wear a red parka over a silk gown!" She eyed him with unfeigned horror. "Don't be ridiculous."

"Me? You're the one being ridiculous. You'll freeze."

"Hardly," she scoffed. "I'm going from a warm house to a warm car to a warm building."

"But the baby—"

"Is safely cushioned from minor temperature changes, and I refuse to make a spectacle of myself. I already feel strange enough."

"Strange? Why?"

"Well . . . maybe *strange* is the wrong word. You see the kind of fund-raising affairs I go to are things like our church's Strawberry Festival or the Humane Society's annual Valentine's Day Dance. The people I'll be mixing with at your affair . . ." She gestured helplessly.

"Are exactly the same types you'll find at your affairs. A few of them are very good, a few very bad, and the vast majority fall somewhere in between. Besides, we'll be sharing a table with Amanda and her date. You'll like her."

I will? Lucy wondered. Why would she like Amanda? Because he did? A sudden spark of jealousy flickered through her. What . . . ? She frowned as she suddenly remembered something. Wasn't his first wife's name Amanda?

Lucy shot a sideways glance at Andrew as he helped her into his low-slung Porsche. Amanda wasn't all that common a name. Could this Amanda they were going to have dinner with be Andrew's ex-wife? Lucy automatically fastened her seat belt as for one wild moment she actually considered claiming to be sick and opting out of the evening. It was an impulse she promptly squelched. She wasn't *that* much of a coward, and besides, even if this woman did turn out to be Andrew's ex-wife, she wasn't the one carrying his baby.

It only took two minutes in Amanda's company for Lucy to discover that she was indeed Andrew's ex-wife—an ex-wife he appeared to be extremely fond of. It was an emotion Lucy couldn't share. Irrationally, she loathed Amanda on sight; loathed her classical blond beauty, the gorgeous designer dress that hugged her lush figure, and most of all, the free and easy camaraderie she shared with Andrew.

The fact that Amanda treated her with open friendliness didn't change Lucy's mind; it merely made her feel guilty. Try as she might, she couldn't match Amanda's sophisticated approach to the situation. And as the evening progressed, the strain of trying began to take its toll. By the time dessert had been cleared away, her head was pounding and her stomach felt queasy.

"What's the matter, Lucy?" Andrew whispered as the waiter filled Amanda's coffee cup.

"Things are getting to me a bit," she whispered back. "But it's all right. I'll be fine."

"It's not all right. I have no intention of allowing you to sit through a bunch of after-dinner speeches if you're feeling sick. Come on." He got up and, taking her arm, practically lifted her out of her seat.

Lucy was torn between relief that she was being offered a way out of such an emotionally loaded situation, and self-disgust that she didn't have the backbone to sit it out.

"Did I miss something?" Amanda watched in surprise as Andrew draped the shawl around Lucy's shoulders.

"Lucy isn't feeling well." To her infinite relief, Andrew didn't mention her pregnancy. She had no idea how Andrew's ex-wife would react to the news, and she had no desire to find out. She was having enough trouble dealing with her own emotions. She most definitely didn't feel up to dealing with Amanda's. And she might very well have some because it was obvious that the woman still had some feeling for Andrew, even if it wasn't clear exactly what that emotional attachment was. All Lucy knew for certain was that it made her feel threatened, and that in turn made her feel confused.

"Goodbye, Lucy. It was nice to have met you." Amanda said with every evidence of sincerity.

Lucy smiled at her, but made no effort to resist when Andrew hurried her out of the ballroom.

It wasn't until she was safely back in her own living room, pretending to sip the decaffeinated tea Andrew had insisted on brewing for her that she felt calm enough to try a bit of probing about the relationship between Andrew and his ex-wife.

"Amanda looked nice in that dress she was wearing," Lucy offered tentatively, with her eyes fastened on his face in an attempt to gauge his reaction to her praise.

"Uh-huh," he muttered, in the midst of yanking off his tie. Lucy watched, temporarily distracted as his jacket, cummerbund and shoes followed. He then unfastened the first three buttons on his shirt, rolled up his sleeves and, sinking down beside her on the couch, propped his black-stockinged feet up on the coffee table.

"That's a relief." He took a swallow of the brandy he'd poured himself.

Maybe for him, Lucy thought ruefully as she took a sip of the tea to dispel the sudden dryness in her mouth caused by the weight of his body tipping her toward him. The warmth from his skin was sending out tendrils of heat to ensnare her already agitated senses, and she fought valiantly against the attraction. There was too much she wanted—needed—to know for her to give in to the almost overwhelming urge she felt for closer physical contact with him.

"The color of Amanda's dress really complemented her fair complexion," Lucy tried again.

"Amanda has a fantastic eye for color," Andrew said approvingly. "It comes of her being an artist."

"Artist?" Lucy frowned, trying to remember what had been said over dinner. "I thought she did something high-powered in advertising?"

"She does. She's a junior partner in one of New York City's top advertising firms." Andrew's voice was casual, and try as she might, Lucy could read no sign that he felt anything more than the pride of one friend in another's accomplishments. It simply didn't make any sense. Every single divorce she'd observed over the years—and she'd seen plenty—had been accompanied by a great many bitter feelings. So why wasn't Andrew's? Because he was still in love with Amanda? The thought chilled her, and she shivered involuntarily.

Andrew casually put his arm around her shoulders and pulled her up against him—an action that threatened to derail her train of thought. But she refused to be sidetracked. She had to know how Andrew felt about his ex-wife.

"From artist to advertising executive is quite a leap. How'd it happen?" she asked.

Andrew took another swallow of his brandy and then said, "I guess it was my fault."

"You don't like artists?"

He chuckled. "No, I liked eating. You see, Amanda and I met in a design class during our freshman year of college. We started dating and by our senior year we were planning on marrying."

"Yes?" Lucy murmured encouragingly when he paused.

"I wanted to wait until I'd finished. It takes five years to get an architectural degree, you know, but Amanda said she didn't want to wait. So we worked out our grand master plan." He laughed self-mockingly. "Amanda was going to get a job and support us while I finished my degree and established myself. Then she'd quit, and I'd support us while she established herself as a portrait painter."

"She was having trouble finding a job when a friend of her father's offered her an entry-level position in his advertising firm."

Andrew shrugged and the movement caused his arm to brush against her breast. Lucy clenched her teeth against the sensation and focused instead on his words. She was eager to learn everything about his past that she could. It would make it easier for her to judge how he would relate to the baby, she decided, thus rationalizing her intense interest.

"The rest, as they say, is history. Amanda took to advertising like a duck to water. She loved it. What's more, she was damned good at it. It wasn't long before she had her own accounts, and she was on the road two-thirds of the time."

"It must have been hard on your marriage," Lucy offered.

"In a sense. We sort of drifted apart over the years until in time we were little more than good friends sometimes sharing the same living space."

"So what changed things?"

"My thirty-fourth birthday. I wanted to have children while I was still young enough to enjoy them. We'd agreed at the start of our marriage that we would have two; but somehow, Amanda never felt the timing was right. Finally, I simply asked her if the time was *ever* going to be right."

Andrew took a long swallow of his drink. "My question forced both of us to face the situation. We decided that while we would probably always care for each other, we didn't love each other and hadn't for years. So we got a divorce."

"Wait a minute." Lucy frowned, trying to understand what he was telling her. "You're saying your marriage was basically happy?"

"I think it might be more accurate to say that it wasn't unhappy," Andrew said.

"Then if you want children and you don't have a lot of negative emotional baggage hanging around your neck from your first marriage, why on earth didn't you simply remarry?"

"I tried," Andrew replied in a goaded voice. "For three years I tried. But the problem was that the women I was drawn to emotionally and intellectually were all career women."

Lucy frowned, remembering that he'd made several vaguely derogatory remarks about her career. "Why is that a problem?"

"Because career women are much too busy to have kids. And even when they do have them, they dump them on a nanny and go on as before, and the child suffers."

"That's a gross oversimplification," Lucy replied emphatically. "Just because both parents work is no reason to assume the child is going to be any worse off than if the mother stayed at home. A second career in the family simply involves a lot more planning."

"Hah!"

"It can work, and work quite well," Lucy insisted. "I have a career that I have no intention of giving up simply because I'm going to have a child. I'd go nuts sitting around the house all day long."

"But you can have your child with you," Andrew argued. "So it isn't the same thing at all."

"Tell me, if you're so against career women being mothers—"

"I'm not," Andrew objected. "I'm simply against a career woman raising my child."

"You lose," Lucy announced flippantly, trying to disguise the pain that shivered through her.

"No," Andrew replied slowly. "Actually, I think I win."

Lucy searched his eyes, seeking a clue to his cryptic words, but she couldn't find one. So she decided to press for more information while he was willing to talk.

"Tell me, Andrew, why didn't you simply marry some girl still young enough to be malleable and fashion yourself a modern-day version of June Cleaver?"

"I tried," he admitted sheepishly. "But do you have any idea how wearing it is to try to make conversation with some girl in her early twenties? They haven't done anything or seen anything. They simply haven't experienced enough of life to be interesting. At least to me."

"You gotta take the bad with the good," Lucy pronounced unsympathetically.

"Not when it would entail sitting across the breakfast table from it for the next thirty years. That's when I came up with my surrogate scheme."

"'Scheme' is right," she muttered.

"It's no different from what you were doing," Andrew defended himself. "You were laying down cold, hard cash for the father to give up all rights to his baby."

"It's not the same," she muttered. "I'm the mother."

"So where is it written that a mother automatically loves a baby more than a father?"

"Well, it isn't," Lucy conceded. "But you must admit that most men aren't all that involved with their children."

"I am not most men," Andrew stated emphatically.

"No, you're not, are you?" Lucy admitted. "In fact, Andrew Killion, I strongly suspect that you're unique." Impulsively, she leaned forward and pressed her lips to his.

Nine

What she had intended to be a casual salute never came off. Instead, when her lips met his, they seemed to cling. Instinctively her eyelids slid shut as she savored the feel of his mouth and the faint taste of brandy that lingered there, slowly seeping into her mind.

Andrew's arms closed around her and he lifted her across his lap.

Lucy squeaked in surprise at her momentary sense of disorientation and then tensed as she felt the muscles of his hard thighs pressing into her soft hips. A joyous sense of rightness filled her that he should be as affected by her nearness as she was by his.

She snuggled closer to him, nestling her head against his shoulder. The slightly musky aroma of his skin filled her nostrils, and the raspy texture of his chin brushed over her forehead. Driven by her need to touch him, Lucy slipped open the rest of the buttons on the front of his shirt and pushed her hand inside.

A satisfied smile curved her lips as his heartbeat accelerated, throbbing into her palm.

Slowly, as if she were exploring unknown territory, she pushed her fingers through the thick pelt that covered his chest. The crisp hair tickled her palms, heightening her sensual awareness of him, and she pushed deeper to feel his slightly damp skin.

Lucy pressed her lips against the hollow at the base of his neck and licked lightly. The taste of salt flooded her mouth.

Andrew trembled at her caress, and he grasped her chin, tilting her head back.

"My Lord, you're incredible," he whispered hoarsely.

Lucy stared up at him, fascinated by the sensuous curl of his mouth. The light from the floor lamp beside the couch poured down over his head, giving each strand of dark hair a glittering white cast. He looked as if he'd been doused with fairy dust. She reached out and touched his hair, her fingers slipping through its short, silky length. Her head fell back against his shoulder, and she tugged him closer, making no attempt to disguise her growing desire. She wanted him to kiss her. She needed to kiss him—needed it with a compulsion that was escalating with each passing second.

"I want you to kiss me." She voiced her demand aloud.

"Not half as much as I want to." Andrew's mouth covered hers. He thrust his fingers through her hair, holding her head steady while his lips exerted pressure. Her mouth opened and he quickly took advantage of the fact as his tongue surged inside.

A series of tremors chased over her skin, making her tremble beneath the force of the desire buffeting her. The flavor of the brandy he'd been drinking was stronger now, and the alcohol burned across her taste buds, further melding her mouth with his.

She was so caught up in his kiss that she didn't realize what his fingers were doing until he'd unflicked the last button on her bodice and pushed it aside. The cool air felt good on her burning skin and Lucy moved languorously, reveling in the sensation. Her languor was abruptly shattered as his hand closed over her breast.

Lucy gasped at the feel of his slightly rough palm against her satiny skin. He rubbed the roseate tip of her breast with his thumb, and the nipple tightened into an aching bud.

Andrew greedily drank the inarticulate sounds of pleasure coming from her lips and began to trace concentric circles around her breast with a warm finger, driving her mindless with longing. Her pregnancy had made her breasts so sensitive that his action was almost unbearable.

Andrew lifted his head and stared down into her face, and Lucy's breath caught at the brilliant glow in his eyes.

"You're so beautiful," he crooned. "Like a piece of fine porcelain that was suddenly imbued with life. And you're mine."

The primitive satisfaction in his voice momentarily shook her free from the sensual thrall that had held her. She frowned at his possessive words, uncertain whether she liked them or not. She'd always felt that people belonged to themselves, not to others—not even to "significant others." But somehow, with Andrew, she wasn't so sure anymore— about a lot of things. There was a thread running through their relationship that had a decidedly primitive cast to it. But before she could explore the thought, Andrew lowered his head and captured her taut nipple in his mouth, and she was much too busy feeling to think—experiencing the shattering waves of pleasure that surged through her, stamping out the rational part of her mind and freeing her emotions to soar to heights she hadn't even suspected existed.

Suddenly Andrew stood, setting her on her feet and supporting her pliant body against his hard frame.

"My beautiful angel." He covered her face with warm kisses as his hands pushed her dress off her shoulders. It fell in a slither of silk to puddle in a bronze-colored heap around her feet. Her slip quickly followed.

"So gorgeous," he whispered, cupping her hips and pulling her into the cradle of his hips so that she was left with absolutely no doubt as to the state of his arousal.

His reaction to her femininity filled her with an exultant sense of triumph, and she boldly followed his lead, pushing his shirt off his shoulders.

Her breath caught in pleasure at the sight of his broad shoulders. Wonderingly she ran her fingertips across his smoothly muscled skin. He seemed so much bigger without the concealing cloak of clothing—bigger and much more dangerously male, as if he'd somehow shed the trappings of civilization along with his clothes. But it was a danger that exhilarated her, making her feel vibrantly alive.

Lucy rubbed the palms of her hands across his chest, shivering slightly as his body hair activated millions of her nerve endings. Slowly, learning by touch and not sight, she explored his shoulders. She traced over his collarbone, dipped into the indentation at the base of his neck and then ran her hands down over his muscular forearms. All that swimming had certainly paid off, she thought dreamily. Andrew had a fantastic body.

Her hands moved lower, running along his waist just above his belt. A shudder shook his frame, and Lucy was suddenly gripped by an unreasoning impulse to goad him into losing his control.

She glanced up at him, catching and holding his bright blue gaze as slowly, ever so slowly, she unbuckled his belt and began to unzip his trousers.

By the time she'd tugged his pants free to fall at his feet, there was a damp sheen on his skin. Impatiently Andrew stepped out of his trousers and kicked them aside. He swept her up in his arms and laid her down on the sofa.

Kneeling beside her, he ran his hand down her body in a sweeping caress that excited her unbearably. His hand came to rest possessively on her slightly rounded abdomen, but his attention was focused on her breasts.

As if savoring the moment, he slowly lowered his head and began to nuzzle first one breast and then the other. Lucy could feel the fluttering warmth of his breath on her burning skin, and she felt herself going limp, totally boneless.

His mouth moved lower still, pausing to lick her navel, and Lucy jerked in reaction. His fingers trailed lightly over the juncture of her thighs, creating a tantalizing friction against the nylon of her panty hose. Her breathing was coming in short gasps that echoed harshly in her ears.

"Andrew!" she moaned.

"It's all right, my darling," he murmured, mistaking the cause of her agitation. "The book says making love is fine until the last month." Andrew's fingers shook as he quickly yanked off her panty hose and tossed them aside. His own briefs were similarly disposed of, and he pulled her into the middle of the sofa and crouched above her.

He lowered himself so that just the tips of her breasts were engulfed in the thick pelt of hair on his chest, and he slowly rubbed back and forth. Sharp stabs of pleasure raced through her at the delectable sensation, and instinctively she grasped his shoulders, trying to intensify the feeling. He felt so good, so right beneath her questing fingertips.

"Do you have any idea how erotic I find the thought of my child growing in you?" he murmured.

His words broke through the sensual haze that held her captive and a moment of doubt shook her. Was Andrew's interest in her generated more by what she was—the mother of his child—than who she was—Lucy Hartford with a unique identity of her own?

She peered up at him uncertainly. His dark hair had been disheveled by her fingers; his eyes were shut as if his mind were totally centered on some inner vision; the muscles in his neck were tightly corded and his face was set in rigid lines.

A warm glow surged through her, dissolving her fears. Andrew looked like a man in the grip of an intolerable tension. There was no way he could be faking emotion that deep.

With no more hesitation, she reached for him, pulling him down to cover her flushed skin. "Now," she demanded imperiously.

"Yes, most definitely, yes," he muttered, shifting between her legs.

Lucy's breath caught in her throat as she felt the hot, blunt length of him probing her damp softness. Suddenly impatient with his restraint, she arched upward, engulfing him.

Her fingers bit into his sweat-dampened skin as tremors of pleasure eddied through her. She hadn't fully absorbed the incredible sensation when Andrew slipped his hands beneath her hips and began to move with short, hard thrusts.

Lucy squeezed her eyes closed, her whole being focused on the incredible pressure building in her. Nothing else mattered but that she attain the release his sure movements were promising.

When it finally came, the intensity of her reaction took her by surprise. Her whole body clenched and then exploded in a starburst of pleasure that left her mindless. She was aware of nothing else. Not of Andrew's muffled shout as he found his own release, not of the weight of him pressing her into the couch nor of the cool air of the living room on her sweat-slick body. Nothing had any meaning outside the very narrow confines of her own emotions.

She heaved a sigh of repletion, closed her eyes and fell asleep with the suddenness of a candle being extinguished.

She didn't resurface until the next morning when she rolled over and encountered a hard body in bed beside her.

Her eyes flew open in shock, and she found herself staring into Andrew's eyes. His unfathomable eyes, she realized as she searched them for a clue to his mood; but it was impossible to read any emotion in his face. Did he regret having made love to her? she wondered. But her uneasiness had no time to grow as he leaned over and dropped a gentle kiss on the tip of her nose.

"Good morning, Lucy." He smiled, and his face creased into deep laugh lines that helped to dispel her fears.

"Good morning, Andrew." She stared at him, still curious as to what he was thinking.

"Why did you make love to me last night?" She inadvertently voiced her doubts aloud and then wanted to crawl under the covers in embarrassment. Of all the juvenile-sounding questions, she thought in self-disgust. While she was at it, she might as well have asked him if he still respected her.

Andrew studied her flushed face for a few minutes and then asked, "Why did you let me make love with you?"

Lucy blinked uncertainly and muttered, "What?"

"Why did you let me make love *with* you?" he repeated. "Nothing was done to you. It was done with you. We were partners."

Partners? Lucy savored the sound of the word. It sounded good. Solid, enduring and comforting. At least when viewed from her perspective. The problem was, she didn't know how he viewed it. She hadn't reached the age of thirty-five without having learned that men's thought processes were at times totally inexplicable, and that usually, those times involved strong emotions.

"I made love with you because I wanted to," she finally said, not wanting to reveal her own feelings without at least some clue to how he felt.

"I see." He eyed her thoughtfully for a few seconds. "I suppose that's enough to be going on with," he finally responded.

But going on where? Lucy wondered in exasperation. Talk about cryptic statements... She tensed as she felt his large hand cup her breast, and her eyes flew to his. The hot glow she saw there drove out all thoughts of what his words might mean. At the moment his actions were much more interesting, and totally unmistakable.

"How's your stomach?" Andrew whispered against her lips.

"Fine," she muttered, more concerned with other parts of her anatomy.

"You're sure?" he persisted. "I don't want to make you sick."

"What you're making me is frustrated." She clutched his shoulders and tried to pull him closer.

"We can't have that, now can we?" He slipped a hand under her and flipped her over onto him.

Lucy's eyes widened as she felt his hard body beneath her. She shifted slightly, savoring the feel of his hair-roughened skin and told him, "I think I'm on top of the situation."

"I have news for you, darling." He rubbed his knuckles across her sleep-warmed cheek. "You are about to become totally immersed in the situation."

"Promises, promises," she taunted, and then gasped as he reached up and pulled her head down to his. Her teasing disappeared in a fiery burst of passion that shot through her, and she willingly gave herself up to it.

"Hey, lady. Come on. I'm running late, and I still got to assemble it." The deliveryman's impatient voice broke into Lucy's discussion with a customer.

"Oh, that's all right, Lucy," her customer said. "You go ahead. I think I'll take your advice and use two strands of the fingering-weight mohair. I'll just pick out my colors. There are so many to choose from."

"Take your time." Lucy gave her an encouraging smile and turned to the deliveryman. "Exactly what is it you need that Annie can't . . ." She paused as her memory suddenly clicked into place. "Aren't you the man who brought my bed?"

"That's right, lady. From Winthrop's Department Store. And now I got your treadmill."

"Treadmill?" Lucy repeated blankly. "I didn't order a treadmill. Nor do I need one. This store is a perpetual treadmill."

"Yeah, I know you didn't order it." He shoved the bill of lading at her. "It was that boyfriend of yours that ordered it, just like the bed. And to think I used to bring my wife candy and flowers when we was going together."

Boyfriend? Lucy felt a warm flush tint her skin. Is that what the garrulous deliveryman thought Andrew was? Her boyfriend?

What a tame, old-fashioned word. *Boyfriend* didn't begin to describe his relationship to her. It was much more convoluted than that. And becoming even more so with each passing day.

"Lady!" The man's exasperated tone penetrated her thoughts. "I do have other stops this afternoon, you know."

"Sorry." With an effort, Lucy brought her attention back to the annoyed deliveryman. "You can put it in the back room where you put the bed."

She signed the bill of lading on the clipboard he shoved at her and then turned to a waiting customer. By the time Lucy had helped the woman pick out three coordinating colors that she liked, the man from Winthrop's had left.

Lucy, curious about the treadmill, wanted to go look at it but a sudden influx of customers kept her busy. It wasn't

until almost an hour later that things were quiet enough for
her to examine her gift.

It turned out to be a lot bigger than she'd expected. It
used up almost all the free space between the end of the bed
and the back wall. All that was left was a three-foot corridor down the center of the room. The sooner they got
started on the addition, the better, she thought.

"What do you think?" The sound of Andrew's voice
from the doorway made her jump.

"That it's a very bad idea to sneak up on people," she
said, with a tartness that didn't entirely disguise the pleasure she felt at seeing him. Hungrily her gaze skimmed over
his heavily muscled body, which was still encased in one of
the immaculately tailored gray suits that comprised his work
wardrobe. His face was set in indulgent lines, and Lucy experienced such a surge of happiness from just watching him
that it worried her. She was becoming much too fond of
him; and that could signal all kinds of problems in the future.

"I wasn't sneaking," he defended himself. "Besides, this
is a store."

"This is a store*room*," she corrected. "And thank you for
the treadmill, but I have a couple of questions."

"Hmm?" He perched on the edge of her desk and Lucy's
eyes were drawn to the way the light gray fabric of his pants
stretched across his thighs. Her fingers itched to touch him
as she remembered the hair-roughened texture of his skin
and the feel of the hard muscles beneath.

"Questions?" he prodded.

"Yes." She forced her wayward mind back to more
mundane matters. "Why a treadmill, of all things? Is this
some kind of editorial comment on my life-style?"

"You mean a Freudian slip?" His eyes gleamed with
laughter. "I plead not guilty. It was bought strictly for exercise purposes."

"But why? I've been walking faithfully. Every evening."

"Sure. You walk right down to that French bakery half a mile away, have a drink and a pastry full of saturated fat, and then you walk home. Any benefit your body might derive from the exercise is lost in the junk you're consuming. And speaking of consuming junk, I brought you something."

He handed her the package he was carrying. It was a large gold-foil-wrapped box.

Lucy cautiously opened it, not trusting his gifts. They all seemed to be heavily imbued with an "It's good for you" motif.

To her surprise, the box contained chocolates.

"Why, thank you." She beamed at him and popped one into her mouth.

"You're welcome." He smiled back. "I was a little worried about the amount of saturated fat you were eating and my doctor recommended those. Not only are they virtually fat free, but they're free of preservatives, too."

Lucy's eyes widened as the flavor of the pseudochocolates attacked her taste buds. She swallowed, gulped and then swallowed again.

"I've got a news flash for you, Andrew Killion." She hurried over to the small refrigerator and extracted a bottle of mineral water to wash the flavor away. "They not only took out the fat and the preservatives, they also took out the taste. That travesty masquerading as chocolate ought to be banned."

"You don't like them?" He looked disappointed.

"Perceptive little soul, aren't you?" she remarked dryly. "Why don't you just leave my dietary habits alone?"

"But you've started to eat a sensible breakfast."

"In case you've forgotten, the sensible breakfast was in exchange for not being bugged about the rest of my diet. You are reneging on the deal."

"You'll live longer if you eat better," he insisted.

"You call ingesting that—" she waved a dismissing hand at the candy "—living? Only if you've got a full-blown case of masochism."

"It isn't that bad."

"Have you had any?" she demanded.

"I don't eat sweets," he answered smugly.

Lucy grimaced. "God deliver me from virtuous people."

"I didn't say I was virtuous." His slow smile set her heart to beating faster. "I merely said I didn't eat sweets."

"Umm, yes. Well, now, about this treadmill." She made a determined effort to turn the conversation to less emotionally fraught pathways.

"Yes, the treadmill." Andrew walked over to it and studied the levers on the control panel attached to the handlebars. "Besides keeping you away from that bakery, it should come in handy this winter when it snows. You'll be able to exercise without fear of slipping on the ice."

"Lovely. Something to look forward to," she commented ruefully.

"Not only that, but you can pick your own speed. From a gentle amble to a brisk walk. Get on and I'll show you. The man in the store demonstrated it for me."

Lucy cautiously stepped onto it, and he pulled a switch, starting it.

Lucy had no trouble moving in time to its snail-like pace.

He pushed the lever forward a little more and the pace quickened slightly.

"You know, Andrew, this may have possibilities. One of the things I hate about walking is that not only is it lonely—"

"If you'd let me move in with you, you'd have company," Andrew inserted.

Lucy looked into his eyes, unbearably tempted even though she was perfectly aware of the fact that she'd be trading short-term pleasures for long-term heartache. If only those short-term pleasures weren't so alluring.

"I told you, you don't need to move in—you're always underfoot. And as I was saying, walking is boring and time-consuming. But with this I could do my walk while I watch the lunchtime news," she said enthusiastically. "Thanks, Andrew. This was really a great idea!" She leaned over to drop a quick thank-you kiss on his cheek, but her lips seemed to cling of their own volition. The slightly rough texture of his skin caused a shiver to vibrate through her.

She tilted her head back and looked into his eyes, fascinated by their huge black pupils, each surrounded by a shrinking blue ring.

"I haven't thrown up in almost three weeks," she told him.

"That's to be expected. The book says—"

"It should have said that discretion is the better part of valor, but what I was referring to was the fact that you quit wearing cologne for me, and I don't think it's necessary anymore," she announced, curious about what type of fragrance he normally wore.

"I still think I'll wait," Andrew replied. "I don't want to give you a relapse."

"All this exercise is more likely to send me into a decline," she said tartly, gesturing down at the treadmill. Her hand accidently caught the control lever and flipped it to maximum. It jerked forward, sending Lucy tumbling backward.

Andrew grabbed her, pulling her up against him. Holding her steady with one hand, he reached around her and flipped the machine off. "You hit Brisk Walk," he explained.

"Brisk walk! For what? A horse? That was more my idea of a mad dash." She made no attempt to move out of his arms.

"My poor angel." Andrew brushed his lips across her cheekbone. She could feel an answering rush of heat beneath her skin. "But don't worry. By this time next year you'll be absolutely fit."

"Or dead," she muttered, locking her gaze on his firm mouth. She pressed closer to his hard body, her eyes never leaving his lips. She wanted contact with those lips—needed it as an addict craves a fix. Unconsciously, she moistened her lower lip with her tongue. It was all the encouragement he needed. His arms tightened around her waist and he pulled her closer.

Lucy sighed in anticipation as his lips met hers. Her mouth opened beneath the pressure he was exerting and his tongue surged inside, stroking sensually against hers.

She pressed closer, finding an exultant joy in his body's instinctive reaction to her.

"Lucy, have you—" Annie's voice pulled Lucy up out of the depths of the erotic whirlpool she was slowly sinking into and she turned, staring blankly into Annie's embarrassed face.

"I'm sorry," Annie apologized. "I didn't realize you were . . . were . . ." Her voice trailed away.

"It's called kissing," Lucy said ruefully. "And there's no reason to apologize. I take it you need help?"

"No, just some more of that cardinal-red worsted-weight yarn from Reynolds." Annie squeezed past them, hurriedly got the box she needed and left.

Lucy stepped out of Andrew's arms and took another swallow of her mineral water, when what she really wanted to do was to pull his dark head down to hers again.

"I think the sooner we get started on the addition, the better." Andrew unwittingly echoed her own earlier thoughts. "It'd be nice to have some privacy. And the book says that the middle trimester of your pregnancy should be the easiest on you. You're past the morning sickness, and you haven't reached the bulky stage yet."

"I don't have the slightest intention of becoming bulky." Lucy looked down her nose at him. "A little rotund, perhaps, but never bulky."

"I weighed ten-and-a-half pounds at birth," Andrew offered.

"What!" Lucy eyed him with unfeigned horror, her mind balking at a baby that size.

"Ten-and-a-half pounds," Andrew repeated. "And from all accounts, I was a healthy kid."

"You should have been. From the sound of it, you were already a couple of months old. I'm going to have a little girl. A dainty little girl of about six pounds."

"Speaking of the baby..." Andrew picked up the portfolio he'd set down on her desk when he'd first come in and handed it to her. "Take a look at this."

Lucy wondered what it was. Nothing she wanted to see, she decided after a quick look at Andrew's face. He looked faintly wary and very determined, as if he were preparing for an argument.

An argument she was more than willing to give him when she opened it and found designs for a child's room, obviously done by an interior decorator.

"You know, I always used to like Winnie-the-Pooh," she remarked levelly.

"It will make a great nursery," Andrew replied with a cautious look at her.

"My daughter is going to have yellow rosebuds on white wallpaper, a white wicker bassinet, a white lace-canopied crib, and sunshine-yellow carpeting. Not this...this red monstrosity.'' Lucy gestured disdainfully at the drawing. ''All that red would make her look like she's living in a bordello.''

''Don't be ridiculous,'' Andrew snorted. ''Bordellos don't really have red carpets.''

''And you'd know?'' she scoffed.

''Better than you. At least I was in one once.''

''Andrew Killion!'' Lucy gave him a look of shocked horror that was belied by the laughter in her eyes. ''I never thought you were that kind of man.''

''I was barely nineteen, and curious,'' he muttered.

''Was it interesting?''

''Who knows?'' Andrew shrugged. ''I lost my nerve, and cut and ran.''

Lucy chuckled. ''Maybe there's more Methodist in you than first meets the eye. But that doesn't change the fact that that color is garish.''

''Stimulating,'' Andrew corrected.

''It'll stimulate our poor little baby right out of her mind.''

''But—''

''Yellow rosebuds,'' she repeated emphatically.

''You are the most stubborn female!''

''Me! Stubborn?'' Lucy hooted. ''You have a corner on the 'stubborn' market.''

''I—''

''Say,'' Lucy interrupted him. ''I have an idea. Why don't you buy her an assortment of those cute little stuffed bears that come in all the bright primary colors?''

''That is not the answer,'' Andrew insisted.

''You've already gotten your answer.'' Lucy gave him a level look. ''It's not my problem if you don't like it.''

''Oh, I give up!'' He grimaced in annoyance.

"Is that a promise?" She grinned at his aggravated expression, having no intention of backing down. No baby of hers was going to spend its babyhood being assaulted visually.

Ten

"Get him!" Andrew yelled.

Lucy looked up from her knitting and squinted at her TV set. "From the amount of blood on his jersey, I'd say they already got him," she observed judiciously. "I wonder how they get the bloodstains out?"

"Bah, what's a little blood? They just lost five yards!"

"Most common sense they've shown all night," Lucy remarked. "Who wants that muddy piece of turf, anyway?"

"You don't understand." Andrew groaned as the quarterback was thrown for a loss again.

"On the contrary, I understand all too well." She glanced around for her cable needle. Not finding it, she thrust her fingers under Andrew's hard thigh, thinking that it might have rolled beneath him.

Andrew turned as she pushed farther and stared at her in bemusement.

"Did I miss something?" he asked.

"I can't find it," she muttered in frustration. "Would you stand up?"

He chuckled. "But if I move you might miss it altogether. Here." He slipped his hands beneath her arms and gently lifted her onto his lap.

Lucy stiffened in surprise at his action, and then a soft sigh escaped her as his body began to work its insidious magic on her.

He smiled at her. "Isn't that better?"

"Better, yes," Lucy said honestly. "More productive, no."

"You don't need to be productive." He began to gently rub his hand over her back, and Lucy felt the first wispy tendrils of desire slip through her receptive mind. "If you want a sweater, I'll buy you one."

"Nine-tenths of the pleasure of the sweater is the fun I have knitting it. Besides, what else would I do while you indulge your bent for organized mayhem? At the rate I'm going, I should have an entire wardrobe done by the time the season's over. When is the season over, anyway?" She leaned her head back and peered up into his face.

"College football on New Year's Day, more or less."

"One can hope less," Lucy muttered, shivering slightly as he shifted her closer, tucking her head beneath his chin.

"The pro season ends a few weeks later, although if the Jets don't get their act together and win next week, their season might as well be over. And speaking of the Jets, would you like to come to my apartment on Sunday and watch their game?" Lucy tensed as he began to nuzzle the skin behind her ear. "Somehow we always seem to wind up at your house, but I'm perfectly willing to play host."

A tremor raced through her as his tongue darted out to taste her soft skin, and she sighed voluptuously. "With the emphasis on playing, no doubt?" Her laugh developed a shaky quality as Andrew slipped his hand beneath her blouse, deftly unfastened her bra, and cupped her breast.

She leaned forward, intensifying the exquisite sensation of his roughened palm rubbing across it. She was going to miss her almost daily contact with Andrew when she flew to the West Coast on Wednesday. Over the past several weeks their relationship had developed at a rapid pace, deepening on all levels—not just the physical. Andrew had begun to share more than just his surface thoughts with her. He was allowing her glimpses of the man behind the sophisticated mask he normally wore; and they were insights she had come to cherish.

"I'm afraid—" Lucy punctuated each word with a quick kiss along his jawline "—that I can't."

"But I was planning a great halftime show." Andrew's eyes gleamed with mischief, and Lucy felt an answering clutch of excitement twist her stomach. She sighed in unfeigned regret.

"Much as I'd love to, I really can't. I won't be here. I'm leaving for Los Angeles on Wednesday and I won't be back until Monday."

"Los Angeles!" Andrew stared down at her as if she'd just announced that she was going up on the next space flight. "You can't go to Los Angeles."

Lucy frowned in confusion. "Of course I can go. I've already got my ticket."

"Los Angeles isn't safe," Andrew insisted. "It's full of gangs and smog and earthquakes."

Lucy eyed him incredulously. "Los Angeles isn't safe? Remember where you live? New York City. The original den of iniquity."

"That's different," Andrew muttered. "I'm with you here. I won't be in Los Angeles. I don't want you to go."

Disturbed at his unexpected response, Lucy slowly climbed off his lap and made a production out of pouring herself a cup of tea from the pot on the coffee table. She was uncertain what to say to him because she wasn't sure what had caused his reaction. He had long since given up his demand that she move in with him so that he could monitor her pregnancy. And he'd never made any attempt to control her movements. So why was he coming unglued about her going to Los Angeles? He couldn't be against airplanes—not after having been on as many as he had since she'd first met him.

Lucy said, "Actually, if the truth were told, I'm not at all that keen to go, either."

"Then don't."

"It isn't that simple, Andrew. I'm going to a yarn and needlework fair to see and order all the new yarns for next summer. Plus, the fair organizers hold a lot of very helpful seminars geared for the small yarn-shop owners. I really can't afford to miss it."

"But anything could happen. You're pregnant!"

"I noticed that." She smiled at him, but he didn't smile back.

Lucy studied the stubborn set of his jaw and sighed. "Andrew, be reasonable. Anything could happen right here. And it's not like I'm some flighty kid. I'm thirty-five years old."

"And pregnant," Andrew repeated.

"Which shouldn't be a problem," Lucy insisted. "The morning sickness is completely gone. And so is the overwhelming tiredness. And my doctor says that air travel is safe until the last six weeks."

"Air travel is never safe!" Andrew shot back. "If you have to go, wait till next week when I can go with you."

"Andrew, you aren't listening to me," Lucy responded patiently. "The yarn fair is this week."

"And you were going to just sneak off without a word to me?" He got to his feet and began to pace back and forth.

"I was not sneaking anywhere." Lucy kept her calm with an effort. "And if I remember correctly, this whole harangue started because I *did* tell you."

"This is not a harangue!" Andrew yelled.

"Well, you could have fooled me!" Lucy snapped back.

He roughly pushed his fingers through his dark hair and, taking a deep breath, he repeated, "Lucy, I don't want you to go."

"I have to," she said, forcing herself to resist the appeal darkening his eyes. She couldn't allow herself to be pushed into agreeing to something that she knew was bad for both herself and her business, and Andrew had no right to ask it of her. She was an intelligent, responsible individual, and most emphatically did not need a keeper—even one she was very fond of. She shied away from examining just how fond of Andrew she was, knowing that the answer would do nothing for her peace of mind.

"Of all the stubborn . . ." He glared at her.

"I prefer 'tenacious.' And if you're going to behave like a thwarted child, I think I'd also prefer to be alone."

"If you were alone, I wouldn't give a damn," Andrew said furiously. "But it's my child that you're insisting on taking with you."

"Go home!" Lucy yelled, finally losing her temper. "And take your stupid ball game with you." She hit the Off button on the remote control.

Andrew gave her a tight-lipped glare of frustration and, without another word, stormed out of the house.

Lucy listened to the sound of the front door slamming behind him and then released her breath on a long, shuddering sigh. She already regretted their argument, but she knew she couldn't give in. She had to go to the yarn fair. And she would. She set her lips together in determination. She'd go and she'd learn all she could from the seminars, look at all the new summer stock and place her orders. And what's more, she'd have a good time. Just as she always did.

As a prophecy it was only partially correct. She did go, refusing to even acknowledge the continuing silence from Andrew, let alone respond to it. She found the workshops were as informative as they always had been—particularly the one on how the recent tax laws affected small businesses—and she was enthralled by some of the new cotton yarns the European manufacturers were showing. But emotionally, her time was a wasteland. Instead of socializing with the fair attendees as she normally did, she found herself spending her evenings alone in her hotel room thinking of Andrew. It wasn't until Saturday night, when she burst into tears as she discovered a college football game while flipping through the TV channels, that she finally admitted to herself just how much she missed him. Surprisingly, though, that very admission had the effect of stiffening her backbone.

She wasn't some die-away ninny to be reduced to tears because a man, even one as special as Andrew Killion, disapproved of her independence. She was a thirty-five-year-old businesswoman; and if Andrew couldn't live with it, that was his problem, not hers. She certainly wasn't about to start altering the way she lived her life and ran her business because she was pregnant with his child. This pregnancy wasn't going to last forever—and then where would she be?

Andrew would undoubtedly transfer all his attention to their child, and she'd be on the outside looking in. His reaction to her going to Los Angeles had shown her quite graphically that even though he might like her, it was the baby he loved. Far better that she face the fact now instead of suffering a sudden break right after the baby was born.

Buoyed up by sheer determination, Lucy threw herself into a frantic round of social events, so that by the time she returned to New York late Monday afternoon she was exhausted as well as late. She'd spent two hours sitting on the runway at the Los Angeles airport while the mechanics had struggled to close the airplane's door, and then another hour on the ground at JFK while a different set of mechanics had struggled to get the same door open. She finally escaped, almost four hours behind schedule and vowing to go by train next year.

The taxi driver who drove her home through the deepening twilight took one look at her wan features and carried her luggage to the front door.

Lucy watched him pull away, bemused at the unexpected courtesy and then, with a weary sigh, unlocked her door and was met by the most delicious odor of baking chocolate.

She blinked in confused surprise. Either Andrew had tossed over his health-food craze or some burglar was making free with her kitchen. Either seemed about as likely, and she had no intention of going inside until she knew for certain whether Andrew had used the key she'd returned to him after the night she'd locked herself out.

"Who's there?" she called out.

"Who do you think it is? Julia Child?"

She felt a wild surge of excitement at the dry tones of Andrew's voice.

"Where have you been?" he demanded. "Annie said your flight was due in at three-fifteen."

"Ha! What's a scheduled arrival time to the airlines?" She reached for her luggage to give herself something to do, when what she really wanted was to fling herself into his arms and kiss him.

"I'll get them." Andrew gently pulled her inside and, reaching around her, picked up her cases, setting them inside and closing the door behind her.

He put his hands on her shoulders and stared down at her pale face, his lips tightening at the dark smudges beneath her eyes.

"Welcome home, Lucy." He dropped a brotherly kiss on her cheek that exasperated her. She might be looking rather the worse for wear, but a real kiss could only help her emotional state. But she lacked the self-assurance to make demands. She kept remembering how much she'd missed him; and that made her feel vulnerable, which in turn made her feel uneasy.

"Thank you, Andrew." Lucy reached out and ran her fingertips over his cheek, relishing the feel of his warm skin. "I missed you," she whispered.

"I missed you, too," he said slowly. "But I'm glad you went. It made me face a few things."

"Oh?" Lucy queried, wondering what he meant. There was no clue to be read on his face. As she watched, his eyes lightened.

"But first, I have a couple of surprises for you." He gave her a pleased grin.

"That's nice," she murmured cautiously, having suffered through far too many of his gastronomical horrors to ever greet one of his surprises with wholehearted enthusiasm—despite the delicious smell of chocolate that filled the house.

"Um, I'm not very hungry at the moment," she told him, trying to pave the way for a refusal without dampening the pleased expression on his face.

"The main surprise isn't food." Andrew helped her out of her coat, carelessly tossed it on the hall table and then urged her toward the stairs. "The best surprise is up here."

"Oh?" Lucy felt a slither of excitement ripple through her. Could he possibly mean... To her disappointment he didn't go into her bedroom at the top of the stairs. He opened the door to one of the spare bedrooms.

With a curious look at his face in which eagerness and apprehension seemed to be about equally mixed, Lucy walked in and then came to a surprised halt.

When she'd left on Wednesday, the room had been a small cubicle with no particular beauty except in her own imagination. That was no longer true. Lucy looked around in shock.

Someone—and logic told her it could only have been Andrew—had completely remodeled the two small rooms on this side of the hallway into one large bedroom. Not only that, but he'd added two huge dormers complete with six-foot windows and window seats.

She swallowed the tears that suddenly clogged the back of her throat as she saw the massive bouquet of yellow rosebuds sitting on the bureau.

"I had a bathroom with tot-size fixtures and a raised tub installed, too." He gestured toward a door that hadn't been there when she left.

"Oh, Andrew." Lucy's voice cracked, and she walked over to the bouquet and gently rubbed her fingertips over a velvety petal. "How on earth did you manage to get all this done so quickly?"

"Contacts, and it wasn't all that hard. There were no major structural changes involved. All I did was open things up a little."

Lucy stared helplessly at him. She'd missed him so much—missed his sharp wit, his keen sense of humor, the way he seemed able to understand what she meant even when she had trouble articulating it. She'd even missed his eternal nagging about natural foods and his inexplicable fascination with football. And yet, now that she could actually reach out and touch him, she couldn't seem to.

"You don't like it?" He frowned, and Lucy hurried to reassure him.

"I love it. It's . . ." She gestured at one of the three-foot long window seats. "It'll be absolutely perfect for a child to curl up in and dream." Tears pricked the back of her throat again. "And a private bath and roses and..." Her lower lip wobbled. "And I know you hate rosebuds, but..."

"Nonsense," Andrew replied bracingly. "I don't hate them, and with all this light and a bright yellow carpet, it'll be fine."

Lucy blinked, blinked again, and then to her horror burst into tears—tears she valiantly tried to stem, but her tiredness made that impossible.

"My poor darling." Andrew scooped her up in his arms and carried her into her bedroom. He set her down on the bed and lay down beside her, gathering her into his arms.

Pressing her head against his shoulder, he gently ran his hand over her hair, brushing it back from her hot forehead.

"Don't cry," he coaxed. "You'll wind up with a stuffy nose and a headache."

Lucy sniffed, tilted her head back and stared at him. "Would you still like me if I have red eyes and sniffles?" she asked.

"Of course," he answered promptly. "What you look like outside isn't nearly as important as what's inside."

"Oh? You mean the baby," she said flatly.

"No, I don't mean the baby." He traced over the bridge of her nose, sending a melting shower of sparks through her. "The baby's only a temporary addition. What I'm referring to is you. And you are one hell of a lady, Lucy Hartford."

"Thank you." She wiggled closer to his hard body.

"Of course, you have a few rough edges that need working on..." His eyes gleamed with mischief.

"Me!" she hooted. "Ha! That's a good one. You'd provide a do-gooder with enough raw material for a lifetime project."

"And would you be willing to take on the project?"

Lucy frowned slightly. His words were teasing, but there was an underlying tension in his features that made her wonder if, perhaps, she hadn't missed something. But her speculation was forgotten as he moved slightly, bringing her up against his hardening masculinity.

A powerful surge of longing hit her, completely banishing both her tears and her curiosity. At this moment, nothing had any meaning except the physical reality of Andrew and her reaction to him.

She closed her eyes and pressed closer, luxuriating in the feel of his body.

"Lucy..."

"Andrew, I told you once before that actions speak louder than words." She lost patience with his desire to talk. She wanted him, not a conversation.

He chuckled. "If that's true, then our actions must be positively deafening." He peered down into her face and asked, "You sure you aren't too tired for this?"

"Making love with you invigorates me," she said honestly.

"Well, in that case..." He covered her lips with a rough eagerness she found more compelling than the smoothest technique in the world. It was as if he'd been holding himself on a tight rein and her admission had provided the key to release him.

Joyfully, Lucy opened her mouth beneath his and welcomed the thrusting warmth of his tongue. Shivers cascaded down her arms at its abrasive friction and she hurriedly fumbled with the buttons on his shirt, pulling it open. She was starved for the taste and feel of him, and it was a lack she was intent on filling.

She pushed her hands inside his shirt, pressing her palms flat against his chest. She could feel the heat pouring off his skin and the escalating rhythm of his heartbeat.

She looked down, fascinated with the way his dark hair curled around her pale fingers as if it were trying to trap her there. His flat, masculine nipples were barely visible in the thick cloud and, curious, she leaned closer to touch one of them with the tip of her tongue.

Andrew jerked as if he'd just been shot. Lucy glanced up at him through slitted eyes and a small, secretive smile curved her lips at his absorbed expression. He looked as if he were caught in the grip of an intolerable emotion. She studied the bunched muscles along his tightly clenched jaw with a growing sense of exultation. He looked every bit as tense as she felt! And if she had her way he was going to look a lot more tense, she vowed.

Her fingers went to his belt buckle and she unfastened it, then unhooked his pants. She glanced up at Andrew to find him watching her with total concentration—as if she were the focus of his whole world.

With infinite care, she pulled down his zipper and began to explore the taut muscles of his flat abdomen with her lips. Her tongue dipped into his navel, and the slightly salty taste of his skin flooded her mouth.

"I can't stand any more of this." Andrew jerked to his feet.

"You, sir, have a very low threshold of frustration," Lucy teased, her voice slightly unsteady.

"Only where you're concerned." He yanked off his clothes, tossing them negligently aside.

Lucy's eyes widened appreciatively at the picture he made, standing beside her bed wearing nothing but the enveloping cloak of his desire for her—a desire that had hardened his face into chiseled planes and stiffened his body into the epitome of masculinity.

She trembled yearningly as he reached for her, disposing of her clothes with none of the finesse she normally associated with him. It was as if what he was feeling had burned away his surface sophistication, leaving the raw essence of the man beneath.

"You are so beautiful, Lucy." His voice was unsteady as he sank down beside her on the bed. "Your skin has the same velvety texture as a pale pink rose petal." His hand swept from her thigh to her breast and Lucy gasped at the heat that flared to life at his touch.

He cupped the soft mound and flicked his thumb over her nipple, teasing it into a tight bud.

Lucy watched in breathless anticipation as his head moved lower and his mouth latched on to the throbbing peak.

Her fingers clutched his head, holding it against her. She clenched her teeth against the agony of emotion he was so effortlessly arousing in her.

"And when you add to all that the fact that you're carrying my child . . ." Gently he stroked the soft bulge at her waist. He lowered his head and nuzzled the swollen skin.

Lucy gasped as she felt her entire body clench in response. "Andrew," she gritted out, an intolerable longing coloring her voice.

He raised his head and stared blindly at her as if his vision were focused elsewhere.

Lucy grabbed his sweat-dampened shoulders and tried to pull him over her. She needed him now. She felt as if she'd been without him for a lifetime, not merely a few days.

"Yes. Oh, yes." Andrew apparently agreed with her haste, for he raised himself on his forearms and, carefully positioning himself above her, entered her with a slow, steady movement.

Lucy wrapped her legs around his waist and, closing her eyes, surged upward. She could feel her skin heating beneath the force of the sensations rocking her.

Andrew grasped her chin in his hard fingers and, covering her lips with his, began to move with sure, gentle thrusts that almost immediately brought her to a climax.

She buried her face in the damp skin of his neck as her breath came in short, broken gasps.

At last, when her tumultuous sensations began to fade, Andrew slipped his hand beneath her hips and began to move again. Lucy's eyes shot open as she felt her body begin to tighten in response to his powerful movements. To her shock she was once again engulfed in a pleasure so intense, she felt consciousness slipping away from her.

Long, long pleasure-filled moments later, she opened her eyes to find herself sprawled beside Andrew. A smile curved her lips at the expression of complete contentment on his relaxed face. He looked like a consummate hedonist who'd just found perfection.

A feeling of fierce pride filled her as she realized that she'd put that look there. She, Lucy Hartford, had totally satisfied this sophisticated, complex man.

"You look like a smug, self-satisfied cat," she murmured.

He raised one eyelid and peered at her. "A tomcat, I sincerely hope. I—" His second eyelid shot open and he frowned.

"What's the matter?" she asked as he jackknifed up.

He turned her slightly and ran gentle fingertips along the side of her right breast. "What's this?" he demanded.

"You don't know!" Lucy eyed him with mock astonishment.

"This is no laughing matter," he reproved her.

"I think it's hilarious," she chortled. "You haven't even got your basic anatomy down yet."

"My anatomy's fine. It's yours I'm worried about. The side of your breast's all red."

"It is?" Lucy tried to look, but she couldn't see clearly. Climbing out of bed, she peered in the full-length mirror on the back of her bedroom door. She frowned. He was right. There was a red mark. She tentatively traced over it and then lost interest when Andrew's image appeared in the mirror behind her.

He reached out and pulled her back against him.

Despite her feelings of sensual satiation, Lucy felt an involuntary twinge of desire at the picture reflected in the mirror: of his leanly muscled, deeply tanned body with her own much paler one held captive against the hand he had splayed possessively across her abdomen.

Lucy closed her eyes as she felt his body also beginning to react to the image. She wiggled enticingly against him.

"Stop that," he muttered, distracted in spite of himself. "I want to know what caused the red mark."

Lucy shrugged, shivering as her action caused her body to rub over his hair-roughened skin. "I don't know."

"Is it sore?" He gently prodded it.

"No," Lucy answered, shuddering at his touch.

"Have you bought larger bras since you've been pregnant?" he demanded.

"I haven't had a chance yet."

"That's probably it. You've grown and your old ones are squeezing you. We'll buy some tomorrow."

Lucy looked in fascination as his mirror image bent its head and began to kiss the soft skin at the back of her neck.

Watching him while at the same time feeling him was an incredibly erotic experience, and Lucy gave a long, shuddering sigh of pleasure.

"I have to talk to you," Andrew said in low tones.

Lucy turned in his arms, captured his head and pulled it down to her. "Later," she murmured against his lips.

It wasn't until almost two hours later that Andrew returned to the subject he'd tried to bring up.

Lucy had just finished a piece of the delicious brownie he'd baked for her as a peace offering and was slowly sipping a cup of hot chocolate, when Andrew suddenly got to his feet and began to pace across her kitchen.

Surprised, Lucy stared at him, wondering what had happened to shatter his mood of contentment.

"We have to talk," he stated roughly.

A premonition sent an icy shiver of fear down her spine and she felt a surge of anger at Andrew for spoiling her happiness.

"So, talk," she replied flatly.

"I've been thinking..." He ran his fingers through his thick hair. "These past couple of months since I've met you..."

He ground to a halt, and Lucy's sense of apprehension grew. What was the matter with him?

"What I'm trying to say is that I think we ought to get married," he finally blurted out.

"Married!" Lucy's apprehension mushroomed into an anguished feeling of hurt misery. So that was why he'd made love to her with such shattering sweetness. To convince her to marry him. And if she did, no doubt she'd quickly find herself relegated to the sidelines of his life, once he gained his real objective: unrestrained access to his child.

"No!" she blurted out from the depths of her own anguish, barely aware of the answering pain that flashed across his face at her blunt refusal.

"But—"

"You don't want me!" she yelled at him. "You just want the baby!"

"Lucy—"

"Oh, go away. Go on!" she screamed, her furious disappointment finding an outlet in words. "Get out!"

Andrew—after one hurt, frustrated look at her—left. And Lucy promptly burst into tears, feeling as if she'd just lost something infinitely precious.

Eleven

Lucy took a deep breath and willed her queasy stomach to behave. The totally unexpected scene with Andrew last night had reduced her emotions to a jumbled mess that was beginning to make itself felt in her stomach.

Her fingers tightened around her cup of herbal tea and she stared blindly out her kitchen window into the weak November sunshine. If only he hadn't sprung his proposal on her like that. If only she'd had some warning, she could have handled the situation better. She snorted in self-disgust. She'd have been hard-pressed to have handled it worse. She'd gone and blurted out a refusal like some outraged Victorian maiden.

Lucy patted the infinitesimal bulge above her navel and sighed. Poor little lamb. She shuddered to think what the baby would turn out to be like with both of its parents behaving as if they had the intelligence of a cabbage.

So think, she ordered herself. It wasn't easy. Her head still throbbed from the seemingly inexhaustible supply of tears she'd shed last night.

She pushed away her untouched bowl of cereal, and that made her want to cry all over again. All those disgusting little bits of mutilated grain reminded her of Andrew, and that reminded her of how she'd told him to get out.

Lucy sniffed disconsolately. Suppose he stayed away? Fear made her stomach lurch, but she faced it anyway. She had to think things out. She'd done enough wallowing in emotional excess last night and what had it gotten her? Nothing besides a monstrous headache, swollen eyes and a red nose. She looked like an understudy for Rudolph the Red-Nosed Reindeer, she thought with self-deprecation.

Lucy took another sip of her tea and forced her mind back to last night. Everything had been absolutely wonderful right up until Andrew's startling offer.

She'd been so glad to find him waiting for her. Those five days had seemed endless without the possibility of Andrew showing up. She had constantly found herself wanting to share a bit of news she'd heard or an interesting happening with him, only to realize she couldn't.

Lucy stared blankly at the polished surface of the oak cabinet above the refrigerator and weighed the depth of how much she missed Andrew. Even in retrospect, it seemed infinite.

Because she loved him. The words seemed to be emblazoned across the cabinet. She blinked and the words disappeared, but the shock waves they'd created didn't. Suddenly it all made sense. Her feelings of tenderness toward Andrew, the incredible sensations she found in his arms, her willingness to compromise with him instead of holding out for what she really wanted . . . All because she loved him. And she'd sent him away when he'd asked her to marry him.

Because he didn't love her, her anguished heart screamed. How could she marry a man she loved to the point of obsession when all he felt was . . .

Lucy frowned, realizing that she didn't know exactly what Andrew did feel for her. He didn't treat her like the embodiment of his feminine ideal. In fact, she grimaced, most of the time he was trying to change her.

Suddenly, as clearly as if her mother were standing in the room with her, Lucy heard her say, "Eat your liver, my precious. It'll make you strong."

Was Andrew's insistent harping on her eating habits and lack of exercise a sign of caring? He hadn't tried to change her. Not the basic her. He'd never said one word of disparagement about her religious beliefs, her political beliefs or her moral code.

Confused, Lucy got to her feet and refilled her teacup from the pot on the counter beside the stove.

Her being pregnant complicated things beyond all belief because she couldn't be positive which of Andrew's actions were a result of what he felt for her, and which were caused by a desire to get his hands on their baby. He *could* even be willing to marry her to get it.

But he hadn't been originally, she remembered. Never once in the beginning of their association had he suggested they marry. Not even when she'd categorically refused to give him their child.

So why had he now? she wondered. Because he'd gotten to know her and honestly believed they could make a go of it for the sake of the baby?

Lucy chewed her lower lip as she considered the idea. As a reason for being married, it fell far short of a declaration of love—even if the man making it didn't fall short in any way.

Andrew Killion was the man she'd always known she'd find if she just waited long enough. And she loved him with all her heart. So what was she supposed to do? she asked herself. Toss away her love in a fit of childish pique because he didn't love her in return?

He liked her a lot. He respected her. He certainly desired her. A warm flush stained her cheekbones at the memory of just how he'd demonstrated that desire.

When you added to all that the powerful lure of their child... Lucy nodded decisively. Their marriage would have a lot going for it. And who was to say that Andrew wouldn't fall in love with her? A feeling of hope bubbled through her. Look how far their relationship had come in just a few short months. By the time she got through wrapping him in her own love, he'd have no choice but to love her in return.

Lucy set down her cup in determination. The sooner she got in touch with him, the better. She picked up her phone and punched in his number, barely able to contain her excitement. To her disappointment, there was no answer at his apartment. Nor was he in his office—at least according to the pleasant-sounding woman who answered.

Lucy thanked her, declined to leave a message, and hung up. She wanted to be the one to call him. She didn't want him returning her call while she was tied up with a customer and wasn't free to talk.

But by twelve-thirty, she was beginning to worry about ever reaching him. She'd gotten no answer to her calls to his apartment, spaced ten minutes apart. Nor had her half-hourly calls to his office accomplished anything more than arousing intense curiosity on the part of Andrew's staff.

Where could he be? she thought in frustration. He wasn't home; he wasn't at work. A sudden fear slithered through her mind. Suppose he'd had an accident on his way home last night?

He'd been upset when he left. Suppose his normal good judgment had lapsed for a second and he'd hit something? Or someone had hit him? An icy weight settled in her chest and her stomach twisted in panic. Suppose a drunk had hit him? There were certainly enough of them on the road these days.

Suppose he was in a hospital somewhere? Or worse? An agonized whimper escaped her. Think! she told herself, deliberately pushing back her fears. If he'd had an accident, there'd be a record of it somewhere. The police would know. Eagerly she reached for the phone book on her desk, only to freeze as she heard the sound of Andrew's voice.

Almost afraid to believe it was really him, Lucy whirled around. Eagerly her eyes skimmed his strong body. It looked intact, if slightly the worse for wear. She studied his pale, strained features with tenderness. He looked as bad as she felt.

Lucy opened her mouth to say something—anything to banish that look—but before she could, he handed her a large manila envelope.

She stared at it and then asked, "What's this?"

"Proof," he said tersely.

"Proof?" Lucy frowned uncomprehendingly. "Proof of what?"

Andrew walked over to the small window and stared out. The harsh noonday light clearly delineated every line in his face as well as the gray tinge to his complexion. Lucy felt a surge of love for him shake her. She wanted to put her arms around him and comfort him.

"Last night..." he began, paused and then continued. "Last night I blew it. I knew how I felt." He grimaced. "Hell, I thought it was obvious. I couldn't bear the thought of you being gone almost a week.

"Did you know I'd arrived at your house right after lunch?" He laughed self-deprecatingly. "I wanted to make sure I saw you the minute you got back."

Lucy stared at him in dawning wonder, hoping he meant what she thought he meant.

He rubbed the back of his neck in frustration. "I meant to woo you gently...."

Lucy swallowed a nervous giggle at the idea of Andrew gently wooing anyone. Actually, she thought with a rising sense of euphoria, she was lucky she'd even gotten asked. It would have been more in keeping with his personality if he'd just ordered her to marry him.

"And I knew if I tried to tell you how I felt after that, you'd never believe me. I'd have to prove it. So I did."

He gestured toward the envelope she still held. "That is a document from my lawyer giving you sole custody of our child. So the baby is no longer an issue between us. And now, I'll ask you again. Will you marry me?" He squared his shoulders and looked at her as if awaiting her judgment.

"You love me," Lucy said wonderingly. "You really love me." A joy so intense it was almost a pain surged through her, and she was too excited to stand still. She wanted to fly.

She flung herself into Andrew's arms, barely noticing when they closed around her with bruising force. "I love you, you angelic man. And I don't want sole custody." She ripped the envelope to shreds. "I want you as involved in our baby's life as I am." She watched with pleasure as the lines exhaustion and worry had carved in his face seemed to miraculously disappear.

"Actually, I'm not really angelic," Andrew corrected tentatively.

"Maybe not the guardian-angel type. But if I remember correctly, the archangels were a pretty feisty lot. You'd fit right in."

"Well, one thing I am certain of..." Andrew looked down at her with such a look of naked love that her breath caught in her throat. "Life with you will be the next best thing to heaven."

Epilogue

"We've got crowning," the obstetrician chortled. "Now, don't push, Mrs. Killion. Pant."

"Pant?" Lucy tried to rally her confused mind.

"Pant. Like a dog. Remember the lessons." Andrew stuck his face directly in front of hers and demonstrated.

"Come on, darling," he urged. "We're almost home."

"Home." Lucy latched on to the word like a talisman. "I want to go home."

"Just as soon as the baby's born, but now you're going to pant," he coaxed.

"Pant." She obligingly tried and then moaned as a tremendous pain encircled her belly.

"I've got the head—" the doctor kept up a running commentary "—and would you look at all that hair?"

Lucy looked at the mirror above her, feeling such a surge of maternal love that tears started to slide down her cheeks.

"Hang in there, darling." Andrew's voice was raw with frustration.

"It's all right," she tried to reassure him. "I just..." More pain gripped her and her words changed to a muffled groan.

"That's one shoulder, two, and we have us a baby!" The obstetrician quickly handed the infant to the waiting pediatrician.

To Lucy's ecstatic relief, the sound of an indignant wail filled the delivery room.

"No problem with this one. Ten out of ten on the Apgar." The pediatrician's words were music to Lucy's ears. He quickly tied off the cord, wrapped the squalling baby in a blanket and laid it in Lucy's eagerly waiting arms.

"Allow me to introduce you to your brand-new daughter." The pediatrician beamed at them.

"A girl?" Lucy looked down at the small, red, wrinkled face in bemusement. "Oh, Andrew, look." She gulped back tears. "Look at our daughter. Isn't she beautiful?"

"The second most beautiful thing I've ever seen," Andrew said reverently.

"The second!"

"You, my darling—" he pushed back her sweat-dampened hair and dropped an infinitely loving kiss on the end of her nose "—are by far the most beautiful thing I've ever seen. If our daughter grows up to be half the woman you are, I'll be satisfied."

"You really don't mind that she's a girl?" Lucy asked hesitantly, oblivious to all the activity around them.

"Of course not!" He looked surprised at her question. "Not only is she a gorgeous-looking baby, but this way you can get all the rosebuds and white lace out of your system so that when our son is born, there won't be any question about him having bright, primary colors."

"I hate to burst your bubble, but the sex of the baby is pretty much the luck of the draw," Lucy felt obligated to point out.

"Not entirely. I found this great book last week that claims you can stack the odds in favor of a particular sex by what the mother eats right before conception," he told her enthusiastically.

"Somehow that doesn't surprise me." Lucy eyed him with loving resignation.

*   *   *   *   *

Now appearing
in a special return engagement, Nora Roberts's
bestselling 1988 miniseries featuring

THE O'HURLEYS!
Nora Roberts

Book 1 THE LAST HONEST WOMAN *Abby's Story*
Book 2 DANCE TO THE PIPER *Maddy's Story*
Book 3 SKIN DEEP *Chantel's Story*

And making his debut in a brand-new title, a very special
leading man... Trace O'Hurley!

Book 4 WITHOUT A TRACE *Trace's Tale*

In 1988, Nora Roberts introduced THE O'HURLEYS!—a close-knit
family of entertainers whose early travels spanned the country. The
beautiful triplet sisters and their mysterious brother each experience
the triumphant joy and passion only true love can bring, in four books
you will remember long after the last pages are turned.

Don't miss this captivating miniseries—a special collector's edition
available now wherever paperbacks are sold.

OHUR-1A

Double your reading pleasure this fall with two Award of Excellence titles written by two of your favorite authors.

Available in September

DUNCAN'S BRIDE
by Linda Howard
Silhouette Intimate Moments #349

Mail-order bride Madelyn Patterson was nothing like what Reese Duncan expected—and everything he needed.

Available in October

THE COWBOY'S LADY
by Debbie Macomber
Silhouette Special Edition #626

The Montana cowboy wanted a little lady at his beck and call—the "lady" in question saw things differently....

These titles have been selected to receive a special laurel—the Award of Excellence. Look for the distinctive emblem on the cover. It lets you know there's something truly wonderful inside!

Take 4 bestselling love stories FREE

Plus get a FREE surprise gift!

Special Limited-time Offer

Silhouette Reader Service®

Mail to

In the U.S.
3010 Walden Avenue
P.O. Box 1867
Buffalo, N.Y. 14269-1867

In Canada
P.O. Box 609
Fort Erie, Ontario
L2A 5X3

YES! Please send me 4 free Silhouette Desire® novels and my free surprise gift. Then send me 6 brand-new novels every month, which I will receive months before they appear in bookstores. Bill me at the low price of $2.24* each—a savings of 26¢ apiece off cover prices. There are no shipping, handling or other hidden costs. I understand that accepting the books and gift places me under no obligation ever to buy any books. I can always return a shipment and cancel at any time. Even if I never buy another book from Silhouette, the 4 free books and the surprise gift are mine to keep forever.

*Offer slightly different in Canada—$2.24 per book plus 69¢ per shipment for delivery. Sales tax applicable in N.Y.

225 BPA JAZP (US)

326 BPA 8177 (CAN)

Name _____
(PLEASE PRINT)

Address _____ Apt. No. _____

City _____ State/Prov. _____ Zip/Postal Code _____

This offer is limited to one order per household and not valid to present Silhouette Desire® subscribers. Terms and prices are subject to change.

© 1990 Harlequin Enterprises Limited

PASSPORT TO ROMANCE
SWEEPSTAKES RULES

1. **HOW TO ENTER:** To enter, you must be the age of majority and complete the official entry form, or print your name, address, telephone number and age on a plain piece of paper and mail to: Passport to Romance, P.O. Box 9056, Buffalo, NY 14269-9056. No mechanically reproduced entries accepted.

2. All entries must be received by the CONTEST CLOSING DATE, DECEMBER 31, 1990 TO BE ELIGIBLE.

3. **THE PRIZES:** There will be ten (10) Grand Prizes awarded, each consisting of a choice of a trip for two people from the following list:
   i) London, England (approximate retail value $5,050 U.S.)
   ii) England, Wales and Scotland (approximate retail value $6,400 U.S.)
   iii) Carribean Cruise (approximate retail value $7,300 U.S.)
   iv) Hawaii (approximate retail value $9,550 U.S.)
   v) Greek Island Cruise in the Mediterranean (approximate retail value $12,250 U.S.)
   vi) France (approximate retail value $7,300 U.S.)

4. Any winner may choose to receive any trip or a cash alternative prize of $5,000.00 U.S. in lieu of the trip.

5. **GENERAL RULES:** Odds of winning depend on number of entries received.

6. A random draw will be made by Nielsen Promotion Services, an independent judging organization, on January 29, 1991, in Buffalo, NY, at 11:30 a.m. from all eligible entries received on or before the Contest Closing Date.

7. Any Canadian entrants who are selected must correctly answer a time-limited, mathematical skill-testing question in order to win.

8. Full contest rules may be obtained by sending a stamped, self-addressed envelope to: "Passport to Romance Rules Request", P.O. Box 9998, Saint John, New Brunswick, Canada E2L 4N4.

9. Quebec residents may submit any litigation respecting the conduct and awarding of a prize in this contest to the Régie des loteries et courses du Québec.

10. Payment of taxes other than air and hotel taxes is the sole responsibility of the winner.

11. Void where prohibited by law.

COUPON BOOKLET OFFER TERMS

To receive your Free travel-savings coupon booklets, complete the mail-in Offer Certificate on the preceeding page, including the necessary number of proofs-of-purchase, and mail to: Passport to Romance, P.O. Box 9057, Buffalo, NY 14269-9057. The coupon booklets include savings on travel-related products such as car rentals, hotels, cruises, flowers and restaurants. Some restrictions apply. The offer is available in the United States and Canada. Requests must be postmarked by January 25, 1991. Only proofs-of-purchase from specially marked "Passport to Romance" Harlequin® or Silhouette® books will be accepted. The offer certificate must accompany your request and may not be reproduced in any manner. Offer void where prohibited or restricted by law. LIMIT FOUR COUPON BOOKLETS PER NAME, FAMILY, GROUP, ORGANIZATION OR ADDRESS. Please allow up to 8 weeks after receipt of order for shipment. Enter quickly as quantities are limited. Unfulfilled mail-in offer requests will receive free Harlequin® or Silhouette® books (not previously available in retail stores), in quantities equal to the number of proofs-of-purchase required for Levels One to Four, as applicable.

PR-SWPS

OFFICIAL SWEEPSTAKES
ENTRY FORM

Complete and return this Entry Form immediately—the more Entry Forms you submit, the better your chances of winning!
- Entry Forms must be received by **December 31, 1990**
- A random draw will take place on **January 29, 1991**
- Trip must be taken by **December 31, 1991**

3-SD-2-SW

YES, I want to win a PASSPORT TO ROMANCE vacation for two! I understand the prize includes round-trip air fare, accommodation and a daily spending allowance.

Name_____

Address_____

City_____ State_____ Zip_____

Telephone Number_____ Age_____

Return entries to: **PASSPORT TO ROMANCE**, P.O. Box 9056, Buffalo, NY 14269-9056

COUPON BOOKLET/OFFER CERTIFICATE

Item	LEVEL ONE Booklet 1	LEVEL TWO Booklet 1 & 2	LEVEL THREE Booklet 1, 2 & 3	LEVEL FOUR Booklet 1, 2, 3 & 4
Booklet 1 = $100+	$100+	$100+	$100+	$100+
Booklet 2 = $200+		$200+	$200+	$200+
Booklet 3 = $300+			$300+	$300+
Booklet 4 = $400+	____	____	____	$400+
Approximate Total Value of Savings	$100+	$300+	$600+	$1,000+
# of Proofs of Purchase Required	4	6	12	18
Check One	____	____	____	____

Name_____

Address_____

City_____ State_____ Zip_____

Return Offer Certificates to: **PASSPORT TO ROMANCE**, P.O Box 9057 Buffalo, NY 14269-9057

Requests must be postmarked by **January 25, 1991**

✂ - - - - - - - - - - - -

ONE PROOF OF PURCHASE

3-SD-2

To collect your free coupon booklet you must include the necessary number of proofs-of-purchase with a properly completed Offer Certificate

See previous page for details